Kirk Smiled
When He Caught Her Staring.

"You don't think I'm underdressed, do you?"

Ava gulped down the rest of her wine.

"Or are you the one who's overdressed?" Humor glowed in his eyes as they moved over her chiffon dress, and he leaned toward her. "Did you need help with the zipper? Or didn't I give you enough time...?"

"Yes...uh, no!" She set her glass down on the small marble table next to the chaise. "Kirk, I'm sorry, but I *am* going to need more time."

The teasing warmth left his eyes. He stared at her a long moment "How much more?" he asked evenly. He'd clearly understood that she hadn't been referring to changing her clothes. "A day? A week? A month?"

"Just until we get to know each other."

He smiled crookedly. "I can't think of a better way for a man and woman to get to know each other than making love."

"That's just it," Ava cried, jumping to her feet. "We wouldn't be making love!"

"Oh, yes, we would!" With one lithe motion he was on his feet."That's a promise."

Dear Reader,

Welcome to Silhouette! Our goal is to give you hours of unbeatable reading pleasure, and we hope you'll enjoy each month's six new Silhouette Desires. These sensual, provocative love stories are both believable and compelling—sometimes they're poignant, sometimes humorous, but always enjoyable.

Indulge yourself. Experience all the passion and excitement of falling in love along with our heroine as she meets the irresistible man of her dreams and together they overcome all obstacles in the path to a happy ending.

If this is your first Desire, I hope it'll be the first of many. If you're already a Silhouette Desire reader, thanks for your support! Look for some of your favorite authors in the coming months: Stephanie James, Diana Palmer, Dixie Browning, Ann Major and Doreen Owens Malek, to name just a few.

Happy reading!

Isabel Swift
Senior Editor

SDRL-7/85

GINA CAIMI
Forbidden Fantasies

Silhouette Desire

Published by Silhouette Books New York

America's Publisher of Contemporary Romance

SILHOUETTE BOOKS
300 East 42nd St., New York, N.Y. 10017

Copyright © 1987 by Gina Caimi

ISBN: 0-373-05338-X

First Silhouette Books printing March 1987

America's Publisher of Contemporary Romance

Printed in the U.S.A.

GINA CAIMI

started making up her own fairy tales when she was six years old. It was the only way she could get through arithmetic class. She sculpts as a hobby, adores the opera, ballet and old movies, but writing remains her major passion. And she still hates arithmetic.

For my father,
whose memories and dreams of Rimini still endure.

One

The huge castle wall gleamed ghostly white in the moonlight. Jutting out from the cliffs, high towers pierced the star-studded sky. With its crenellated battlements, the medieval curtain wall encircled the rocky summit like a gigantic crown. The silhouette of a rugged mountain range was visible in the background; the timeless murmur of the Adriatic Sea followed the stretch limousine up the steep hill.

As the limo continued its solitary climb up the road winding through a forest of ancient oak trees, Ava felt as though she were entering a fantasy world. The authentic thirteenth-century castle of Gradara seemed as unreal to her as a picture in a book of fairy tales. As unreal as the knowledge that she was about to be married in that castle to a man who was little more than a stranger.

"No, absolutely not!" Kirk's words shattered Ava's thoughts. His was no actor's voice; it was rough, yet strangely mellow sounding. A voice that was used to giving orders, confident that they would be obeyed.

"No paparazzi," he spoke into the car phone. "Only members of the media who've received invitations are allowed. I won't have this wedding turned into a three-ring circus. Have the rest of the cast and crew arrived?" He paused to listen intently.

While he went on checking to make sure that the wedding would be as polished a work of art as the movies he produced, Ava studied her husband-to-be with the trained eye of an actress.

She was determined to be as businesslike about the situation as he obviously was, to ignore the anxiety knotting up her stomach, the cold sweat that was making her white chiffon dress stick to her skin. She forced herself to think of him as just another actor she was getting ready to rehearse a love scene with as she searched for qualities in him she could relate to, qualities she might find personally attractive.

Kirk Falconer wasn't conventionally good-looking, she had to admit, but, then, nothing about him was conventional. He was a man who broke all the rules. As a person without much self-confidence, his daring was one thing Ava admired about him—that and his boundless energy.

Even sitting, he seemed to be moving. Though the interior of the limousine was ample, it could barely contain his massive six-foot-four-inch frame any more than the elegant, custom-made evening clothes he wore could disguise his powerful build. There was something of the street brawler about him, an aura of danger beneath his civilized veneer that spoke of a man who'd fought his way out of a Jersey City slum to the very top of his profession.

But the hardships he'd endured to emerge as one of the most successful independent producers in Hollywood had left their mark on him. At thirty-eight, his thick unruly hair was steel-gray. Deep lines etched the corners of his dark, intense eyes and framed the most blatantly sensual mouth she'd ever seen.

She could see how some women might find him attractive. His name, she recalled, had been linked in the gossip columns over the years with some of the world's most famous and desirable actresses. His exploits were legendary in Hollywood.

Ava shifted uncomfortably in the velour seat. She'd never thought of Kirk Falconer as a man; he was more a show business legend. Even before she'd auditioned for him—was it really over a month ago?—she'd been in awe of him. Once she'd landed the leading role in his movie based on the tragic story of Paolo and Francesca, theirs had been a strictly professional relationship. She was stunned when he'd asked her to marry him—no, not asked, ordered.

"I want you to marry me," he'd said bluntly. When she'd told him she couldn't, that she felt nothing for him, he'd laughed. At the time she thought his reaction strange; now she understood it. Kirk Falconer always got what he wanted. And, for some reason, he wanted her. Tonight he would finally have her.

The knots in Ava's stomach tightened until she was barely able to breathe. Turning away, she stared, unseeing, out the car window just as Kirk hung up the phone.

"I'm sorry I was on the phone so long," he apologized uncharacteristically. "I hope you don't mind."

She wondered why what *she* felt should suddenly matter to him. Without looking at him, she managed an indifferent shrug. "I don't mind."

Kirk wasn't taken in by Ava's attempt at indifference. Though she was outwardly composed, her delicate fingers were unconsciously twisting the engagement ring he'd given her as if it were a shackle she was trying to break free of.

Something twisted inside him, as well. Was she having second thoughts about marrying him? Maybe she just didn't like the ring. He knew from experience how much expensive jewelry meant to women, though she'd seemed more surprised than delighted when he'd given her the engagement ring. Maybe she would have preferred a conventional diamond ring instead of an emerald.

He'd been captivated by the emerald the moment he'd seen it. Its color had reminded him of the extraordinary green of her eyes, and when it caught the light it glowed the way her eyes did when she laughed, though she rarely did. Except when she was onstage.

Onstage, her intense shyness fell away and her whole being came alive, sensuous and vibrant, as she gave herself completely to the character she portrayed. He'd always wondered whether she gave herself that completely when she made love. Since the first time she'd auditioned for him he'd wanted to find out.

He wasn't a man given to fantasizing about women, but ever since he'd met her he'd lain awake nights, imagining what it would be like to have her in his bed, to slowly strip away her shyness and have her come alive in his arms. He longed to see her covered only by the luxuriant blue-black hair that spilled down to her waist. Her face haunted his dreams.

He'd known many beautiful women, some even more beautiful than Ava, but none with that undefinable quality she had. With her softly rounded face, large liquid eyes and exquisitely sensitive mouth she might have been the model for a Raphael Madonna. She projected a combination of innocence and sensuality that was as rare as it was irresistible.

He'd never wanted a woman more.

Nor had he waited so patiently for a woman before. He had no illusions about the reason she'd finally agreed to marry him: it wasn't that she loved him. In time, he vowed fiercely, he would also have her love. He always got what he wanted.

"The reason I was on the phone so long," Kirk added when he saw that Ava was retreating behind that quiet reserve she used to keep people at a distance, "was to make sure everything's going smoothly. I want our wedding to be perfect."

"I understand," Ava murmured. She knew that the wedding was merely another Falconer Production to him. He was in the business of creating fantasies, and that was all he cared about. "It'll be great publicity for the film."

"The film?"

"*Paolo and Francesca.*" She was surprised she had to remind him; their lives for the past month had revolved around nothing else. "Making a movie based on the legend of Paolo and Francesca in the castle where they actually lived and died should be good for a lot of press coverage. Isn't that why you wanted to hold the wedding there, too?"

He frowned and she wondered what she'd said wrong.

"It wasn't because of the movie I—" Kirk stopped before he made a complete fool of himself. He thought she'd realized that he wanted to give her a wedding a princess might envy, and make their first day together as husband and wife one she would always remember.

"I don't understand," she said. "Why, then?"

A sardonic smile curved his mouth. "I just thought you'd enjoy getting married in a castle. You should have told me if you preferred a private ceremony."

You should have asked me, Ava was about to say, but didn't. With a resigned sigh, she shook her head. "No, this is fine." Turning away, she stared out the window again. If they had been in love, naturally she would have preferred a private ceremony, but as things were she was glad there would be so many people present. It would make it easier for her to act out the charade. Yet she would still need all the acting ability she possessed.

A wave of sadness swept over her. She'd never expected her wedding day to be like this.

As usual when unpleasant feelings threatened to overwhelm her, Ava retreated into the safe, ordered fantasy world of acting. She concentrated on the moonlit vision of the huge gatehouse, the main entrance through the massive stone wall they were nearing. The gliding motion of the car created the illusion of a tracking shot in a movie. Even as Ava marveled at the strength and beauty of the twin towers standing guard on either side of the gatehouse, the actress part of her mind carefully registered her reactions. She would need them to recreate Francesca's feelings when she saw her husband's home for the first time.

Her fascination deepened when the car eased through the open gateway: it was like driving into another world. The tiny village of Gradara gleamed, unchanged, in the moonlight, looking exactly as it had seven hundred years ago. Medieval houses still flanked the steep cobblestone road, which hadn't been built with cars in mind, and the limo barely missed scraping the white stucco buildings with their sloping, clay-tiled roofs. The purr of the engine was the only sound in the almost eerie stillness.

Through another large gateway at the end of the street they reached a small piazza. The church that dominated the square was dwarfed by the rectangular inner wall and its four corner towers. Through yet another arch they climbed a wide grassy slope where trees studded the base of the fortifications, their autumn branches softly swaying in the breeze. Finally, the castle where Paolo and Francesca became lovers and paid for their forbidden love with their lives rose before them.

La Rocca—The Rock—as the huge, rectangular castle was called by the natives, had three towers of equal size and one massive square tower that was the keep. Small, graceful arches held up the merlons and embrasures, and ran uninterrupted along the corner towers and all along the walls. The walks where soldiers once patrolled were covered with a tiled roof, as were the towers, which rose flush with the top level of the walkways. Only the massive keep, its merlon crown open defiantly to the sky, towered above the battlements. By sheer height and size it dominated the rest of the castle, creating an impregnable fortress.

Kirk was as fascinated with Ava as she was with the castle, and he was filled with an envious longing. He wanted her to look at *him* that way, anticipation glowing in the depths of her wide green eyes, lighting up her face. He ached to be part of the excitement she was feeling, to share it with her. He was surprised and confused by his feelings. He'd never needed to share things with a woman before, but she was unlike any woman he'd ever known. She stirred feelings in him no other woman had.

For one thing, he couldn't stand being shut out by her. "That's extraordinary, isn't it?" he ventured, nodding in the direction of the castle.

"Yes, it is," she agreed, turning toward him. "With all the research we did on medieval Italy, I still wasn't prepared for anything like this." The smile she gave him included him in her delight and made his pulse jump. "It's like a fantasy world."

It suddenly occurred to Kirk that Ava was at her happiest when she was in a fantasy world. What could have happened to her in the short span of her twenty-five years to make the real world seem so unsatisfying?

"I wonder what Francesca's feelings must have been," she went on, her skin as pale as the moonlight flickering across her face, "when she traveled this same road with Paolo, not knowing that he'd married her in his brother's name." A wistful sigh escaped her. "What dreams she must have had about the wedding night to come...the life she believed she was going to share with the man she really loved."

Ava swallowed past the sudden lump in her throat and tears burned behind her eyes. Life still had a way of not turning out the way you expected, she thought bitterly, and men still betrayed the women who loved them.

Resolutely she pushed all thoughts of Derek out of her mind. By submerging her own feelings in what she imagined Francesca's feelings had been on her wedding day she was able to recapture her previous enthusiasm. "Look!" She leaned toward Kirk, pointing out his window. "There's the moat and the drawbridge."

He caught a whiff of the perfume she wore, warmed by her skin. Though he found it arousing, the exact nature of the scent eluded him, as she always did.

"But why are we stopping?" she asked as the limo came to a smooth halt.

"Because we have to go the rest of the way on foot."

In her eagerness to approach the castle, Ava was out the car door before the chauffeur could get there. With barely concealed impatience, she waited for Kirk to join her.

Kirk admired her impulsive enthusiasm; he just wished she were as impatient for the wedding ceremony to begin. "Just a moment, Ava." He had to grab her hand to hold her back.

Ava gasped audibly. Kirk's hand was so large it swallowed up hers completely, so warm it sent shivers up her arm.

Kirk couldn't deny his disappointment when he felt Ava stiffen at his touch. He saw the enthusiasm drain out of her and watched helplessly as she withdrew behind her shy facade. He released her hand as abruptly as he'd taken it and turned to the chauffeur, who was standing at attention beside the car.

"Marco, we won't be needing you again for several hours," he managed in his most businesslike manner. "When you finish parking the car we'd like you to join us at the reception. All right?"

The chauffeur was unable to reply for a moment; he was clearly as surprised by Kirk's invitation as Ava was. Kirk's tone, though as commanding as ever, had held no trace of condescension.

Ava was forced to admit that was how he always dealt with the people who worked for him, from a name actor down to the company gofer. She had to give him credit for that.

"*Grazie*, Signor Kirk," the darkly handsome young man blurted out gratefully when he'd recovered, "but..." With an expressive wave of his hand he indicated his uniform. "I am not in the proper attire for such an occasion."

"You look fine to me," Kirk returned. "Of course, if you'd rather not go, then—"

"No, no, *signore*, I am exceptionally honored," Marco was quick to assure him in his delightful accent. He gave

Ava a frankly admiring glance. "And may I say you are a man as fortunate as you are generous." Whisking off his cap, he bowed his head to Ava. "Miss Kendall, my most sincerest..." He frowned while he struggled to find the proper word, then brightened when he recalled it. "Most sincerest good wishes on your marriage day."

Ava smiled; it was impossible not to respond to such genuine warmth. "Thank... *grazie*, Marco."

"I will see you more later then." Marco bowed his head again before he replaced his cap and slid behind the wheel of the limousine.

"That was a lovely thing you just did," Ava told Kirk as they began walking the short distance to the drawbridge.

"Not really." He dismissed his generosity with a shrug. "Marco's going to be our driver for the duration of the shoot and...well, making a movie, especially on location, everyone ends up being like one big family."

She wondered why he felt the need to explain; he actually seemed embarrassed by his generous gesture. She never would have expected that of him. He was a far more complex man than she'd realized, and that bothered her. One of the reasons she'd finally agreed to marry him was that she thought she knew exactly what kind of a man he was. That knowledge made her feel safe; it made it easier for her to protect herself from him.

"Here's the moat and the drawbridge you couldn't wait to see, milady," he drawled.

Because of her training as an actress, Ava was acutely aware of the most subtle changes of inflection in a person's voice, and she picked up the sarcasm in his, though she couldn't understand the reason for it. She decided to concentrate on the wide dry gulch surrounding the castle, instead. "But there's no water."

"No, of course not. The castle hasn't been used as a fortress for centuries," he explained. "It's an historical landmark now."

"All the more reason there should be water in the moat." She sounded disappointed, as if the castle didn't live up to her fantasies.

What other fantasies did she have? Kirk wondered. He would have given anything to be part of them. "There will be plenty of water when we start filming," he promised her.

A soft smile flickered across her face as she peered down and Kirk knew she was already visualizing the way the moat would look filled with water. Her smile faded suddenly when she looked up, and she took a step back. Silently she stared across the moat at the massive stone walls of "The Rock," looming above them.

"What is it?" He slid her a wry look. "Don't tell me you just saw the ghost."

"The ghost?"

"The natives claim that whenever there's a full moon, like tonight, Francesca's restless spirit can be seen roaming the battlements."

"Really?" A cold shiver went through Ava. She told herself it was from the wind, which made a sound like a drawn-out sigh as it weaved in and out of the battlements—a sigh that could easily have belonged to a soul in torment.

A teasing smile tugged at the corners of Kirk's mouth as he watched Ava. "Do you believe in ghosts?"

"No, of course not," she said, but she continued scanning the battlements with wide eyes, as if she were hoping to see one. "Though I can almost believe that ghosts *do* exist in a place like this," she added. "I read somewhere once that emotions, really powerful emotions like intense love or hate, generate a kind of energy that lingers in the atmosphere of a place long after the people themselves are gone from it."

She turned to look at him, her eyes filled with wonder. With her hair streaming in wild, dark waves around her face, the transparent, shimmering layers of her white chiffon dress swirling around her delicate body, she looked too lovely to be real, like a vision conjured out of dreams.

His dreams, Kirk suddenly realized, dreams he never even knew he had. He longed to grab her and pull her into his arms, to take her mouth in a kiss as consuming as the hunger raging inside him. It took all the willpower he possessed to suppress the urge. The excitement making her eyes gleam like emeralds was not due to him, he knew, and he couldn't bear to see it drain out of her at his touch again. His pride was one thing not even *she* could take away from him.

"I can believe it's possible that the memory of a love as intense as Paolo and Francesca's could still be lingering among these stone walls," she went on, her face struck with moonlight. "Can you imagine how much they must have loved each other when they knew that every time they met they were risking certain death?"

"That's love all right," Kirk agreed wryly. He was just beginning to understand how a man could be willing to risk everything for a woman.

Ava's long, rueful sigh was carried off by the wind. "That kind of love doesn't exist anymore."

"Yes, it does," Kirk insisted, surprised by the bitterness in her tone, the pain darkening her eyes. "It's just that that kind of love is as rare today as it was then. But there are still a few fortunate men and women who love each other that deeply."

Ava stared off into space a moment. "Really?" she murmured as if to herself. "I wonder what it's like to love and be loved like that."

Kirk never would have believed that mere words could be filled with such longing. Reaching out, he brushed a wind blown strand of hair off her face. "I've never known what it's like to love and be loved like that, either," he found himself admitting. Sliding his hand into the thick, dark tangle of her hair, he turned her face back to his. "We could find out what it's like, you and me."

Ava was too stunned to react. With startled eyes she stared at Kirk as if she'd never seen him before. He'd never spoken to her about love. Nor had he ever looked at her that way—no man had ever looked at her with such naked longing.

She felt thoroughly confused, and a bit frightened. Was this the same man who'd boasted he always got what he wanted because everyone had a price and he was willing to pay it? Hadn't he stopped at nothing to discover what her unwilling price was? What did such a man know about love?

"You and me?" She laughed, a single bitter laugh that cut right through him.

"Yes!" It was a vow made in anger and frustration, but one Kirk intended to keep. His hand tightened in her hair. Fiercely, he sealed the vow on her mouth with his.

Ava's startled cry was lost in the hard, possessive crush of his mouth. Before she could recover, powerful arms locked around her, surrounding her, pulling her up against the taut length of his body. His mouth moved on hers with a hunger that took her breath away, forcing her lips apart to admit the hard thrust of his tongue.

A groan tore from him as if he'd been starving for the taste of her. She might have been able to resist his superior strength but was helpless against the longing coiled in every muscle of his body. His tongue searched the warm depths of her mouth with an intimacy that left her shaking. She never would have believed him capable of such passion. A strange molten thrill started spreading through her and there was nothing she could do to stop it.

The uncontrollable shudder that went through Ava reverberated deep inside Kirk. Never had he known a woman to respond to him with such emotion, a purely instinctive sensuality. He could feel her mouth and body heat under his as she melted, soft and vulnerable, in his arms. The sudden rush of tenderness he felt for her took him by surprise. His kiss gentled even as it deepened.

Sensations Ava had only dreamed of swirled through her. Her arms went up to twine around his neck and her body surged passionately against his. Mindlessly she returned his kiss, eager for a love that matched her fantasies. It was only when he dragged his mouth away from hers, breaking the spell she was caught up in, that reality, and what little reason she had left, returned.

The victorious smile curving his lips and gleaming in the depths of his eyes told her how he felt about her response to him. As he stood there towering over her, with his strong uncompromising features and powerful build, he might have been a medieval warlord enjoying his conquest.

But when he spoke, his voice was surprisingly soft and a bit ragged. "I was right, wasn't I?"

"No," Ava returned coldly, pushing away from him. "That's not love."

He laughed—the same way he'd laughed when she'd told him she wouldn't marry him. "Maybe not. But it's a damn good start in that direction."

He turned and stepped onto the drawbridge. "I think we'd better get going." Reverting to his usual cool, efficient manner, he offered her his arm. "It's not considered good form to be late for your own wedding."

An eerie feeling swept over Ava as she let Kirk lead her across the drawbridge. She felt as if she were crossing into a world suspended halfway between reality and fantasy. The ghostly walls of the castle loomed over her, massive towers thrusting high into the dark, silent sky. The wind moaned through the battlements. As they neared the main gatehouse, a sudden strange premonition gripped her: something was waiting for her within those ancient, love-haunted walls. Something that called to her deepest, most secret fantasies.

A kind of fearful excitement shivered through her when they stepped through the iron-bound portal into the fortress.

Two

Ava smiled with delight when she caught her first glimpse of the internal courtyard of the keep. The medieval coat of arms embossed in the stone still proudly proclaimed the castle to be the property of the Malatesta family, lords of Rimini. The fresco of a battle scene beside the entrance glorified their conquests, and the well, which during countless sieges had provided them with the only fresh water available, was barely changed by time. But the rest of the architecture contrasted sharply with the purely defensive exterior of the fortress. An elegant arcade with wide, sweeping arches lined the sides of the courtyard, topped by an open gallery perched on graceful white columns.

"I hadn't expected anything like this," Ava admitted to Kirk while they crossed the open section of the courtyard to the shelter of the arcade. "It's so elegant."

"Wait till you see the house I rented for us," Kirk told her proudly. "It's a villa high up on a cliff overlooking the Adriatic. It was originally built as a summer home for a Renaissance prince."

Ava had barely recovered from his kiss, so she certainly wasn't ready for this new surprise. "But I thought we were going to stay at the Grand Hotel in Rimini with the rest of the cast and crew."

"No, that was just for last night," he informed her. "Once we're married, I'd rather we were on our own."

"On our own?" That certainly was news to her. "What about Mike?"

Kirk frowned, as he always did when he was reminded of Mike's influence on Ava. "Your father will be staying in Rimini with the other members of the cast."

"And he agreed?"

"Agreed?" It obviously hadn't occurred to him to ask. "Where you live is no longer your father's responsibility, Ava," he reminded her dryly. "In less than an hour, you're going to be my wife."

"Yes, I know, but I thought..." She'd thought that the marriage wasn't really going to change things; he'd never given her any indication that it would.

"It's bad enough we're not going to have a honeymoon because the Italian government wouldn't permit a change in our shooting schedule," he informed her. "But the villa is secluded, so at least we can have some privacy. It'll be almost like having a home."

Ava was growing more confused every minute. Knowing Kirk's reputation, wanting a home was the last thing she would have expected of him.

"There are so many beautiful places like this in Italy," he went on, his voice softened with an intimacy she wasn't accustomed to. "Instead of going back to the States after we wrap the film, I thought we'd stay on here for a month." He took her arm as they turned the corner under the sweeping arches, drawing her closer to him. "Venice is only a two-hour drive up the Adriatic coast from Rimini. We could stay there for a week, then go on to Florence and Rome, then over to the Italian Riviera." Anticipation glowed in his dark eyes as they locked with hers. "We'll have a real honeymoon."

Ava had to look away so he wouldn't see how deeply the thought of going on a honeymoon with him—with all that that implied—disturbed her. She could feel the warmth from his hand seeping through the sheer fabric of her sleeve, the shifting muscles of his thighs brushing against hers with every step.

Kirk had meant to tell Ava about his honeymoon plans after the wedding, but the way she'd responded to his kiss had made it impossible for him to put off sharing his surprise with her any longer. "Then we'll cross over to the French Riviera, and we'll end our honeymoon in Paris." His fingers slid down her arm to entwine with hers. "Would you like that?"

His softly possessive touch, and the surprising effect it was having on her, added to Ava's confusion. Nothing was as she thought it would be! "But what about postproduction on the film?" she said evasively, pulling her hand away. "You told me you personally supervise the editing and scoring on all your films."

"This time I'm going to let the director handle it." He came to a halt and his eyes met hers again, humor gleaming wryly in their depths. "I think it's more important that we have some time to ourselves so we can finally get to know each other, don't you?"

He didn't wait for her answer; she couldn't have come up with one if he had. She felt betrayed, as if he'd just sprung a carefully prepared trap on her. He'd led her to believe that their marriage would be a business arrangement, a mere extension of her five-year contract with him. Why had he waited less than an hour before the wedding to tell her about secluded villas and romantic honeymoon trips? The only passion they shared was for filmmaking. Yet his kiss still burned on her mouth and her remembered response burned on her face.

"Here's the chapel we're going to be married in." He pointed to the arched doorway on the right before indicating the elegant marble stairway nearby. "Those stairs lead to the living quarters. Our wedding reception will be held upstairs in the great hall." His hand came to rest on the small of her back. Slowly but firmly, he led her toward another arched doorway on the left. "I've had them set aside this room for you down here, so no one will bother you while you finish preparing."

He'd thought of everything, Ava realized resentfully. She could feel the trap closing around her. Abruptly she halted in front of the open door and spun on her heel to face him. "Kirk, I—"

"Here she is—finally!" a voice mingling relief with exasperation cut her off. A tall, lanky young man came rushing out the door in a highly emotional state. "Do you know what time it is?" he demanded of her, his tone rapidly approaching hysteria. "It's eight-thirty! The wedding is at nine! How can I be expected to do something marvelous with your hair in just thirty minutes?"

"Relax, Leon," Kirk intervened soothingly. "Miss Kendall doesn't need marvelous. The less you do to her hair, the better."

"Really, Kirk!" the hairdresser protested. "I spent the entire flight yesterday and most of last night making sketches. I had the most marvelous medieval creation in mind." Reaching out, he grabbed chunks of Ava's waist-length hair between his long, sensitive fingers. "Don't you realize what I can do with this?"

"I have no doubt," Kirk murmured; he knew what he'd like to do with it. "But there's such a thing as gilding the lily. I suggest you save your creative inspirations for the film."

"You're the boss," Leon sniffed. Releasing the long, blue-black strands of Ava's hair, he waved her frantically through the doorway ahead of him. "Come along."

Ava didn't budge. The hairdresser's frantic demands only added to the feeling that her life was completely out of her control. "Kirk, I must talk to you."

"Time's awasting," Leon reminded her, tapping his foot impatiently on the stone floor.

"Just give us a minute, will you, Leon?" Kirk said with quiet authority.

"Whatever you say," Leon tossed over his shoulder, "but it's now twenty-five minutes to lift-off."

Kirk waited until Leon had disappeared into the impro-vised dressing room before asking, "What is it Ava?"

"Well, it's just that everything happened so quickly with us, and we've never really talked about any of this."

"It's a bit late for that, isn't it?"

"No, it'll only be too late *after* we're married," she in-sisted. "That's why we have to talk about it now." She drew in a long, steadying breath. "Kirk, I've never lied to you about how I . . . I feel about you."

A sardonic smile twisted his mouth. "How you *don't* feel about me, you mean."

"Well, yes," she admitted uncomfortably. She didn't love him, but she didn't want to rub it in, either. "So I can't marry you under false pretenses."

"Neither one of us has claimed anything that we don't believe," he said, feigning an indifference he was far from feeling.

"I know, but you were just talking about going on a month-long honeymoon and..." She was unable to continue.

"I thought you might enjoy it," he drawled. "I know I'd do everything in my power to make you enjoy it." The naked sensuality in his gaze let her know he wasn't referring to sight-seeing.

"That's just what I mean, Kirk," she said in a strained voice. "I can't marry you unless it's clearly understood that—"

"I thought I'd settled all this with your father," he cut her off, his voice hard. "This is hardly the time to make additional demands."

"Additional demands?" she repeated, confused. "I don't know what you're talking about."

Kirk was accustomed to actresses using his power and position to further their careers. He knew that was the reason Ava had agreed to marry him, but at least she hadn't pretended to care for him as the others had. He'd always admired her honesty. Why did she have to start lying to him now?

"I never made any demands," Ava protested, hurt that he would think her capable of such a thing.

Not directly, he knew, but her father had made plenty. "Just tell me what you want, Ava," he said bluntly. "If it's within reason, you can have it."

Ava flinched as if he'd slapped her. It was just like him to think that he could buy her love. She pulled herself up proudly. "I don't want a thing. I was trying to find out what *you* want."

A quizzical smile tugged at the corners of his mouth. That was certainly a new one on him. "What I want?"

"Yes, from me...as your wife," she attempted to explain. "I thought I knew exactly what you expected of me. But after all this talk about villas and honeymoons and...what happened before..." The memory of his kiss swept over her.

Kirk saw fear mingling with excitement in her eyes as she looked up at him; her parted lips trembled softly. She wasn't like the others, he realized with a rush of love. He'd been right about her, after all.

"What I'm trying to say is," Ava went on with difficulty, "I can't marry you unless I know I can give you what you want. What do you want from me, Kirk?"

"Everything." The same hungry demand was in his eyes as they moved over her. "Everything you have to give."

Ava staggered back a step. "That's impossible!"

He laughed. "Maybe, for the time being. I can wait."

"But you don't understand, I—"

"Ava, listen to me," he interrupted, taking her by the shoulders. "Have I ever forced you to do anything you didn't want to do?"

"No," she had to admit. But he didn't have to force her; he had more subtle ways of getting exactly what he wanted.

"I never have, and I never will," he promised softly, drawing her closer.

"But, Kirk—"

"Twenty minutes to lift-off," Leon's voice floated, loud and clear, out the door.

"Damn him but he's right," Kirk muttered. "We're running out of time." His fingers tightened around her shoulders, burning through the delicate chiffon as he pulled her up against him. She lifted her hands to push against his sides and felt powerful muscles contract at her touch.

"Don't fight me," he grated, bringing his face down to hers. "We're going to be fantastic together." His mouth took hers in a quick, fierce kiss. "You'll see."

With that, he spun her around and propelled her into the makeshift dressing room.

"It's now nineteen min—" Leon began before he got a good look at Ava's face as she stood shaking a few feet from the doorway. "What's the matter, lovely?" He started toward her. "Are you all right?"

She managed a quick nod.

"Got the wedding jitters, eh?" A sympathetic smile creased his face, all sharp ironic lines. "Not to worry. Mother Leon's here now." Putting a boyishly slender arm around her shoulder, he walked her over to a portable makeup chair. "I'm going to be your Hair on this picture and you are going to be so gorgeous."

Even in the state she was in, Ava realized that Leon's brash, ironic manner concealed the soul of a pussycat. She appreciated his attempt at getting her to relax, but it wasn't working.

"That creature over there," Leon went on with mock contempt, indicating the petite young woman skimming through a fashion magazine, "is Makeup."

"Hi, I'm Cathy," the pert redhead said, tossing the magazine aside and jumping to her feet.

"We're going to have to work on her at the same time, Red," Leon told Cathy when she stopped in front of the mirror that had been set up on the long, medieval table facing the chair. The three-sided mirror reflected the collection of many hued jars and bottles, the wide assortment of brushes and sponges that were already neatly lined up on a white linen towel. A water glass held a bunch of lilies of the valley.

"No problem," Cathy assured him as she quickly wrapped a plastic cover-up around Ava's shoulders to keep her chiffon dress from becoming soiled with makeup, while Leon began brushing out Ava's hair with long, even strokes.

With the quick, deft movements of professionals, they continued working on her in silence, handling her face and hair as if they were objects apart from her. Once again, Ava felt that her life was completely out of her control. The vaulted ceiling and brooding stone walls of the medieval room added to her feelings of insignificance. A helpless anger began tying her stomach into knots. She might have been a slave girl being readied for her master's pleasure.

She recalled the victorious look in Kirk's eyes after he'd kissed her, the possessive way his dark gaze had moved over her when he'd told her he wanted everything she had to give. But she had nothing to give, not anymore. Derek had taken everything when he'd walked out on her. Everything except the determination never to love a man more than he loved her, or ever again to be at the mercy of a passion she couldn't control.

Ava stiffened when she felt the soft, wet tip of the lipstick brush gliding over her lips. It reminded her of the way Kirk had traced her lips with the tip of his tongue.

"Is it cold?" Cathy asked, referring to the lipstick that had been sitting in the cold, damp room for hours.

Ava shook her head. No, Kirk's tongue had been like liquid fire darting inside her mouth, burning her until her own mouth had caught fire and she'd melted in his arms. She was still shocked by her response to him. She never dreamed he was capable of such passion.

Unlike most of the producers she'd met, his manner toward her had always been respectful and businesslike. That was one of the things she'd liked the most about Kirk—she felt safe with him. She'd agreed to marry him in part because, knowing how he cared only for his work, she was sure he wouldn't make any great demands on her sexually. Now she wasn't so sure.

The knots in her stomach tightened as she thought of the wedding night to come. Suddenly she knew that she couldn't go through with the marriage.

"Hey, hold it a second," Leon protested as Ava bolted to her feet, pulling the plastic cover-up from around her neck as she did. She hadn't realized that he was still winding the last sprig of lily of the valley in her hair.

"Our little bride is getting eager," he drawled suggestively.

"Who can blame her?" returned Cathy with a trace of wistfulness.

Ava couldn't help wondering whether Cathy's wistfulness was the result of a longing for marriage in general or for Kirk in particular.

"Let's have a look at you first," Leon ordered. He took a step back and studied Ava critically. "The son of a so and so was right," he exclaimed when he'd finished admiring his handiwork. "She doesn't need marvelous." Quickly he moved away from the mirror so Ava could see herself.

Leon had made a series of tiny braids on both sides of her head. He'd left a couple dangling beside her face and had twined the remainder around the top of her head; the rest of her hair spilled in long dark waves over her shoulders and back. In between the openings in the braids, he'd wound sprigs of lily of the valley. The delicate, bell-shaped flowers formed a fragrant white tiara, the perfect complement to her flowing white chiffon dress.

"Isn't she ready yet?" Mike's booming baritone preceded him into the room.

"There's your cue, lovely," Leon said, giving his own appearance a quick check in the mirror. "Give 'em hell."

"Good luck." With a warm smile, Cathy grabbed Ava's hand impulsively. "You're getting the best there is, honey."

"Hurry up, Red, or we're going to miss our cue," Leon told her, which sent her rushing after him. "Lights, camera, action!" he called out as they passed Mike on his way in.

Ava's father was wearing his best blue suit, the one he saved for auditions or special occasions. There had been many auditions in his life, she knew, but few special occasions. He looked older than his fifty-two years in spite of the new, youthfully styled toupee he wore. His premature baldness and short stature were merely two of the many disappointments that had etched deep lines in his frail face. His green eyes, which were the only feature she'd inherited from him, glowed with a desperate happiness.

"You've never looked lovelier, princess," he murmured, looking at her as if she were the culmination of dreams he was almost afraid to believe had come true. "I'm so proud of you." His long, sensitive hand, which was clutching her wedding bouquet, trembled visibly. "I've never been more proud of you than I am at this moment."

"But, Mike, I . . ." Ava was about to tell her father she couldn't go through with the wedding, but the words withered inside her when she saw the tears of joy misting his eyes.

"And wait till you see the feast Kirk arranged!" he exclaimed, blinking the tears away. Whenever Mike became excited or emotional, his speech lost its trained, pear-shaped tones and reverted back to its Brooklyn origins. "Everything served on the finest china, with silver, and hand-blown crystal goblets!"

Fresh tears welled up in his eyes, and she wondered how she'd ever be able to tell him her decision.

"You've always been *my* little princess, but Kirk's giving you a wedding fit for a queen." Reaching into his breast pocket, he pulled out a handkerchief and dabbed at his eyes with it. "Wasn't I right about Kirk? Aren't you glad you listened to me now?"

"Mike, I have to—"

"And speaking of royalty," he rattled on enthusiastically. "*I* just had a drink with a real live count. Me, Mike Kendall of Flatbush Avenue." He shook his head at the wonder of it all as he stuffed the handkerchief back in his pocket. "This wedding must have cost Kirk a small fortune."

"I'm sure it's all coming out of the publicity budget," Ava said flatly.

"A small fortune, I can tell you." Mike had a way of not hearing what someone said if it was something he didn't want to hear. "Why the flower arrangements alone must have set him back thousands of dollars." As if he suddenly remembered the bouquet he was still clutching, he held it out to her. "Kirk asked me to give you this."

The wedding bouquet was a cascade of exquisite white roses dotted with lilies of the valley; white roses were her favorite flower. Instead of being pleased, Ava felt even more resentful. Once again, Kirk had thought of everything. Her hand clenched into a fist at her side. "No, I can't," she blurted out. "I can't marry Kirk!"

Thanks to years of calling up emotions on demand, Mike's initial horror quickly changed to laughter. "Come on now, princess," he chided playfully as though she were five years old again and had refused to eat her spinach. "This is just nerves. That's all this is, just last-minute wedding nerves. It's only normal." He laughed again, but his laughter had a hollow ring. "An hour before I married your mother, I was ready to skip town I was so nervous."

"You don't understand. Kirk deliberately misled me." In an attempt to get him to listen to her for once, Ava grabbed her father's arm. "I can't marry Kirk because I don't love him. I could never love him and that's what he wants."

"Ava, Kirk knows exactly what the situation is. We've been through all that. You're forgetting that this is more than a marriage, it's a partnership. This is your big break! Most actors never get that big break and you're going to throw it away, for what? So you can marry for love? Some struggling actor like that one you were involved with?" He paused to give her time to remember Derek. "Is that what you want?"

Ava's hand slid off her father's arm. "No."

"Love," he sneered bitterly. "*I* can tell you all about marrying for love. Your mother and I married for love and what good was it?" With a gesture of futility, he set the bouquet down on the medieval table. "Money, that's what's important. We never had any money because I was always struggling to make it as an actor. When I think of all the crummy jobs I had to take to support my family when all I wanted to do was act, and then—"

"Dad, please," Ava implored. She'd heard all the arguments before; they were the same arguments he'd used to talk her into marrying Kirk in the first place. "I know what you had to give up because of me, but—"

"And then at night, after working all day," he went on, the bitterness pouring out of him, "I'd act for nothing in some off-off-Broadway showcase, hoping and praying that I'd finally get my big break. And even when I did land a part in a legit play, with my damn luck, the play would be a flop. But I wouldn't give up on my dream. Your mother could never understand that." He laughed bitterly, brokenly. "So much for love."

Suddenly he began pacing in front of her, his steps as charged with anger as his words. "You were there. You heard all the arguments." He slanted her an accusing look. "She never forgave me for getting you interested in acting—you know that. You remember all the fights we had because I'd spend what little money I'd saved on you. On acting lessons and dancing lessons, on pretty clothes so you'd look your best when I'd take you on auditions."

The guilt Ava had always felt for being the cause of her parents' breakup ached inside her. "Dad, I know I could never repay you for all the sacrifices you made for me."

"But I never minded making those sacrifices, princess," he insisted, coming over to her. "Because we always shared the same dream. Now, thanks to Kirk, that dream can become reality." Softly, reassuringly, he began carefully stroking her hair as he used to when she was a little girl crying out some childish hurt or disappointment. "A man like Kirk has money and power. But more important, he believes in your talent. He can make you a big star just as I always dreamed you would be." His green eyes grew moist as they looked up into hers imploringly. "It's the only dream I have left."

Ava felt what little resolve that remained drain out of her. Wordlessly she reached over and picked up the wedding bouquet.

"I knew you wouldn't let me down, princess," Mike uttered gratefully. "You're the only one who's never let me down." He laughed suddenly, an almost maniacal laugh. "Just wait till your mother sees you up there on that screen larger than life. And me beside you. I'd give anything to see her face."

"Hey, what's holding up production?" Leon's sardonic voice broke in as he stuck his head in the doorway. "The natives are getting restless, not to mention the bridegroom."

"We were just on our way," Mike assured him, pulling himself up haughtily. "There were a few appropriate remarks I needed to make to my daughter on her wedding day."

"You picked some time to tell her the facts of life," Leon drawled. "I'll let them know they can start the music."

As Leon hurried off, Mike offered Ava his arm in a quaintly formal manner. Grateful for the support, Ava clung to it. Her legs were shaking so much she was sure she couldn't have walked the short distance by herself.

"Don't be anxious," Mike said when he felt her hand trembling uncontrollably. "Rise above it. You're an actress. Remember what I taught you."

Ava was barely able to think. No opening night had ever left her so paralyzed with fear.

"Just make believe this is the wedding scene from the movie," Mike said as if he were directing her in the scene. "I'm your father, Guido da Polenta, lord of Ravenna. You're my lovely and innocent young daughter, Francesca, on your way to marrying Paolo Malatesta, the man you love. Just concentrate on the physical realities of the scene."

Ava concentrated on walking through the arcade in time with the strains of the wedding march that spilled out of the chapel, rushing up to meet her. Moonlight poured through the sweeping arches onto the stone floor, pooling around her feet. "There he is. You see him?" Mike stage-whispered as they started down the aisle in the chapel.

Ava forced herself to notice how the light from the candles on the altar flickered over the intricate designs covering every inch of the walls and the huge arched ceiling, making the gold leaf glitter and dance like flames.

"The man you love is waiting for you there in front of the altar."

But the man who was waiting for her in front of the carved stone altar, the only person in the chapel undiminished by the vaulting Romanesque ceiling, could not have been Paolo Malatesta. With his proud bearing and rough, uncompromising features, he might easily have been Francesca's real husband—Gianciotto Malatesta, one of the fiercest warriors in an age of warriors, the lord of all Rimini.

His eyes met hers from the far end of the chapel and held them every step of the way. Suddenly she was no longer able to lose herself in a fantasy world. Nothing had ever seemed more real to her. She was Ava Kendall. In a matter of minutes, she would be Mrs. Kirk Falconer.

She swayed when her father's arm, as frail as its support had been, was no longer there for her to lean on. It was replaced by Kirk's powerful arm. His gaze moved over her possessively, almost triumphantly, reminding her that she would soon belong to him.

Ava swore to herself that she would never belong to him in any meaningful way.

A slow smile curved his mouth as though he'd read her thought. And suddenly, Ava knew, with a certainty she couldn't understand, that a man like Kirk Falconer would never be satisfied until he possessed her, heart and soul.

Three

———

Congratulations!" gushed the woman who'd just insinuated herself between Ava and Kirk with the ease and grace of a steamroller. If she was aware of cultural attaché Ferretti's annoyed frown at having been interrupted in mid-sentence, she chose to ignore it. "I'm simply dying to meet the blushing bride."

Kirk's perfunctory introductions were unnecessary. Lorraine Landis was as famous as the stars whose private lives she so mercilessly exposed. Because of her reputation, and her particularly long eyeteeth, she was known in Hollywood as "The Vampire." As always, she was meticulously groomed. Her bouffant hairdo was so stiff with lacquer it probably could have withstood a hurricane without having a single champagne-blond curl mussed. The glossy perfection of her makeup added to the mask-like quality of her face. Her features were as sharp as her tongue.

"What a spectacular wedding! A Kirk Falconer production if I ever saw one," she said in her high nasal
twang. She had a way of making a compliment sound like
an insult. "Only you, Kirk, could have thought up something like this." With a sweep of her bejeweled fingers, she
indicated the great hall, where the reception was taking
place. No detail had been overlooked, no expense spared,
in order to recreate a medieval wedding feast.

The walls of the hall were hung with colorful banners.
The wedding party was seated, where the castle family
would have been, behind a long table on a raised platform
at the upper end of the hall. The guests sat on benches at
two vertically placed tables in front of them.

Silver and crystal gleamed in the flickering light. The
thick, wax candles burned in candelabras set at regular in-
tervals along the tables and hung suspended overhead in
large iron loops. Iron wall brackets held flaming torches.
Additional light, as well as heat, was provided by the fire
in the massive stone fireplace, the smoke-blackened spits
empty now of quails and pheasants.

"How romantic to be married in a castle," Lorraine
twanged. "I never knew you were so romantic, Kirk."

"There are a lot of things about me you don't know,"
Kirk returned dismissingly. "Signor Ferretti was just filling us in on the history of the castle." A wicked gleam lit
up his dark eyes. "This should interest *you*, Lorraine. It
seems Lucrezia Borgia once lived here."

"Fascinating." She smiled tightly. "But I'm not much
for history. You don't mind, Kirk, if I borrow your lovely
little bride for some girl talk, do you?" Before either Kirk
or Ava could respond, she put an arm lock on Ava any
wrestler would have been proud of.

"I've been trying to get your attention for hours," Lorraine complained as she led Ava away. "I was just beginning to think you were deliberately avoiding me."

"No, why should I?" Extricating her arm from the gossip columnist's, Ava came to a halt. "It's just that I've been so overwhelmed."

"All this *is* rather overwhelming," she allowed. "You're not used to this kind of luxury, are you?"

"No," Ava admitted unashamedly.

"That explains why you seem so uncomfortable. Why the dinner alone—I never saw so many courses. I ate so much I'm going to have to fast all day tomorrow." She gave Ava one of her tight little smiles; the pointed tips of her teeth protruded beyond the thin line of her upper lip. "I noticed *you* barely touched your food."

Ava hadn't realized that her movements had been so carefully observed, and this shocked and offended her.

"Is that because you're dieting for the film, or has love taken your appetite away?" She made "love" sound like a four-letter word. "What's really bothering you?"

Ava had never had to deal with a gossip columnist before and she wasn't quite sure how to go about it. She forced a smile. "Nothing's bothering me."

Lorraine's icy blue eyes narrowed. "Then why do I get the feeling that something's not quite right?"

"I don't know what you mean," Ava said, glancing nervously over at Kirk.

Kirk was listening to Signor Ferretti, who was busy expounding on Rimini's importance as a seaport since Roman times, while keeping an eye on Ava. When he saw the almost desperate glance she shot him, he quickly excused himself.

"You didn't *have* to get married," Lorraine persisted, "did you?"

"What?"

"You can tell *me*. After all, it's not something you can hide for long." Brazenly the gossip columnist's eyes moved over Ava's body, looking for telltale signs. "Are you pregnant?"

"No," Ava gasped. "But how dare you ask such a question?"

Stopping beside Ava, Kirk placed a protective hand on her arm. "What question?"

"I was just trying to find out your lovely little bride's secret," the columnist purred.

"Secret?" Kirk didn't bother to hide his annoyance.

"The secret of her success," Lorraine replied evasively. She was clearly afraid to tangle with Kirk. "How did *she* succeed in hooking one of Hollywood's most eligible bachelors, when so many more worldly actresses have tried and failed. What's she got that's so special?"

Kirk smiled coldly. "If you knew what it took to make a woman desirable to a man, you wouldn't have to ask that question." He paused to enjoy the stricken look on Lorraine's face. "That's enough questions for tonight."

"Well, of course, if you two have something to hide," she tossed off maliciously when they turned to walk away.

"What did she mean by that crack?" Kirk asked as he was leading Ava back to Signor Ferretti, who was deep in conversation with the Italian countess he'd been actively pursuing since their introduction earlier.

"She thinks something's not quite right with us."

"She always was pretty sharp," Kirk admitted. He slanted Ava a sardonic glance. "But, then, you certainly wouldn't win an Academy Award for your performance as the happy bride."

"I'm sorry," Ava said sincerely. The last thing she wanted was for anyone to know the truth about her marriage. "I'll try to act more—"

"Don't," he cut her off sharply, coming to an abrupt stop. "Don't ever act with me, Ava. It's the one thing I couldn't take."

"Kirk, I didn't mean it that way."

With a silent curse, Kirk turned and walked away. He hadn't meant to behave like an emotional schoolboy. It wasn't like him to lose his cool, but he'd watched her pick at her food earlier as if it were her last meal before her execution. For hours she'd sat at his side, unsmiling, barely speaking. He'd gone to a great deal of trouble and personal expense to make their wedding an experience she'd always treasure, and it meant nothing to her.

"Signor Ferretti, how about that tour of the apartments you promised earlier?" Kirk asked the suave, fortyish gentleman when he'd rejoined him. He had already visited the apartments some months earlier, but Lorraine was still watching his and Ava's every move. He thought it a good way to get out of reach of her prying eyes.

"*Adesso?*" the cultural attaché blurted out, caught off guard. "Now...this moment?" He was clearly reluctant to leave the company of the attractive contessa. Remembering his responsibilities, however, he nodded with a charming smile. "It would be my pleasure to accompany you, Signor Kirk."

Disappointment dimmed the contessa's hazel eyes, but she, too, smiled, the smile of a hostess performing her duties.

With a wave of his elegant hand, Signor Ferretti indicated a candelabra on a nearby table. "It will be necessary to take some light with us."

"Please don't bother," Kirk insisted. He envied them their longing for each other's company. He wasn't used to envying other people. He glanced behind him to see where Ava was. She was standing just a few feet away from him, looking utterly lost.

"I remember the way from the last time I was here, scouting locations," Kirk added. "I know you've seen all this a few hundred times. There's no need for you to go through it again."

Kirk had to turn away from the relieved smiles lighting both their faces. "I'd like to make an announcement," he said loudly, facing the crowd of people talking and laughing, drinking champagne, enjoying the wedding feast as he wished he and his bride were. "For those of you who are interested, we're going to make a tour of some of the apartments in this section of the castle."

Ava's father stopped in the middle of the heated discussion he was having with an English actor involving the method school of acting. "You can count me in."

"That sounds like fun," Lorraine twanged as she hurried over to Kirk as quickly as her stiletto heels would allow.

Within moments, Kirk was surrounded by a dozen or so people, mostly actors from the film and several English and American journalists. The Italian guests, however, had seen it all before and preferred the more modern pleasures of champagne, dancing and the promise of a new romance.

Somewhat wistfully, Ava watched Signor Ferretti and the contessa. They were deep in conversation again, oblivious of anyone else's presence. Though they were speaking in Italian, she didn't need a translator to understand what they were saying. The contessa's face was flushed and her eyes were sparkling, and it wasn't from the champagne.

"Ava, are you coming?" Kirk asked, pulling her out of her wistful daze.

"Yes, of course." She moved quickly to his side. Feeling the columnist's inquisitive gaze on her, Ava gave Kirk a bright smile. He didn't return it.

"All the electric candles in the rooms we'll be shooting in have already been replaced by the genuine article," he explained, "so we'll have to take this with us." Bending over, he grabbed a heavy iron candelabra in one hand, lifting it off the table as easily as if it were made of cardboard. "Just follow me, ladies and gentlemen." He offered Ava his arm in a purely mechanical gesture. Yet she felt powerful muscles stiffen at her touch.

Suddenly she reexperienced the strong crush of his arms, the hungry, burning touch of his mouth. She had to quicken her steps to keep up with his long strides. Effortlessly he held the many armed candelabra up before him, lighting the way. Candlelight spilled over the rough lines of his face and threw his shadow up against one wall of the hallway. His huge shadow swallowed up hers.

The eerie feeling that had gripped Ava when she'd first seen Kirk waiting for her at the altar took hold of her again. He seemed to belong in this harsh medieval world; the high stone walls of the castle diminished everyone but him.

"This is the war and council room," Kirk announced, coming to a halt. Releasing her arm, he threw open the iron-bound door. As though he were the master of the house, he walked over to the long wooden table in the center of the room and set the candelabra down on the intricately carved table next to an hourglass.

"Well, come on in," he ordered with brusque hospitality when they all hesitated at the doorway, disoriented by the dark shadows crawling up the walls.

A shiver went through Ava when she stepped into the room that had nothing to do with the chill permeating it. The wide fireplace that dominated one wall proudly displayed the Malatesta coat of arms on its triangular chimneypiece, which rose clear to the twenty-foot-high ceiling. Normally the only source of heat in the room, the fireplace was unlit. The glistening thick, stone walls exuded dampness. It seemed to Ava that they were dripping with centuries-old tears.

"I know many of you aren't familiar with the story of Paolo and Francesca," Kirk said when everyone had assembled in the room, "so I'll give you a short synopsis." He waited for several reporters to finish digging out notebooks.

"Francesca, who will be played by Ava Kendall," he acknowledged with a nod in her direction, "was the daughter of Guido da Polenta, lord of Ravenna. To seal an alliance between the warring Polenta and Malatesta families, it was agreed that Francesca would marry Gianciotto Malatesta, lord of Rimini." With a wave of his hand, he indicated Larry Davenport, the actor who'd been cast in the part of Francesca's husband.

In response to everyone's attention, Larry took several steps forward, dragging a "crippled" leg behind him while he playfully twirled the imaginary mustache of a silent screen villain. Everyone laughed at his antics—everyone except Ava.

"Now Gianciotto," Kirk went on, "who was also called *lo sciancato*—the cripple—though not to his face, was a brutal man, skilled in the arts of war and power, but not in the gentler art of love. So Francesca's father—"

"That's me," Mike jumped in, thrusting himself center stage. "I'm Mike Kendall. I play Francesca's father in the movie."

Ava had never realized how hungry her father was for attention. He basked in it like a cat in the sunshine. She couldn't remember the last time she'd seen him so happy.

"Knowing how shy and sensitive my young daughter was," Mike rattled on, "I was afraid she'd refuse to marry Gianciotto once she met him, so I concocted a scheme to trick her into it."

"Probably right here in this very room," Kirk said, resuming control. "At a table such as this one."

It was a perfect room for plots and betrayals, Ava thought resentfully as her eyes moved over the severe, thronelike chairs sitting up against one wall as if in judgment. The sheer massiveness of the room, and the austere furnishings gave it a purely masculine look, powerful and unyielding. Love had no place here, nor did a woman. She was certain that this had been the very room where Francesca's father and husband-to-be had plotted to trap her in a loveless marriage.

"So they agreed to send Gianciotto's younger brother, Paolo, to Ravenna, instead," Kirk continued, "to woo and wed Francesca in Gianciotto's name. Unlike his brother, who was dedicated to war and conquest, Paolo was a cultured and elegant young man."

"They didn't call him Paolo *il bello*—the handsome one—for nothing," Mike chimed in.

"Francesca fell in love with Paolo the moment she saw him," Kirk went on, "and eagerly agreed to the marriage. Paolo also fell in love with Francesca, but as he himself had been forced into an arranged marriage when he was seventeen, he had no choice but to carry out his orders. He married Francesca in his brother's name without telling her the truth."

"Good Lord, did that actually happen?" an English reporter asked, looking up from her notes.

"Yes, she was betrayed by all of them," Ava blurted out bitterly. "Forced into a loveless marriage by her father, to a man who considered her a mere possession, abandoned by the only man she'd ever loved...."

Suddenly she became aware of the silence that was as heavy as the shadows flickering across the walls. Only then did she realize the emotional intensity of her outburst. Kirk was staring at her, an undefinable look on his face. It took all her acting ability to recover. "I'm sure you can all imagine Francesca's feelings on her wedding night when Gianciotto came to her bed instead of Paolo."

"By the way, where is Paolo *il bello*?" Lorraine piped up. "We've met all the other leads in the cast."

For once, Ava was grateful for the gossip columnist's compulsive nosiness; that was something she'd been wondering about herself.

"We're having a problem with conflicting dates," Kirk informed everyone smoothly. "I won't know for sure whether the actor I want for the part is free until tomorrow. I have a standby in case he's not."

"But who is he?" Lorraine persisted.

"I don't think I should release his name until I'm sure he's available," Kirk returned. "But I will say he's one of Hollywood's brightest and most dashing new stars."

"You can at least give us a—" Lorraine began.

"Francesca's bedroom is just down the hall," declared Kirk, cutting her off with an annoyed air. Picking up the candelabra, he walked toward the door. "That's where the final scene of our story takes place."

Mixed emotions gripped Ava when she stepped through the Romanesque entrance into Francesca's bedroom. Since she knew of the tragedy that had taken place there, anticipation mingled with a sense of intruding on something intensely private, almost sacred. Somehow she felt that those four walls had been Francesca's only refuge in that male-dominated fortress, that they'd witnessed the only joy and happiness she would ever know. So Ava wasn't surprised to find how different the ambience of the bedroom was from the other rooms she'd seen in the castle. The historically accurate furnishings were a testament to Francesca's spirit.

A colorful heraldic border edged the polished wood-beamed ceiling, and panels of fabric in a richly patterned design softly draped all the wainscoted walls. An elaborately carved canopy bed rested on a carpet whose lush colors hadn't been dimmed by the passage of time. Over an intricately inlaid clothes chest, flanked by two chairs, hung a religious triptych painted on wood, and a gold crucifix caught the candlelight from atop a well-worn prayer bench. Nearby was a book stand upon which a medieval book lay open, as though whoever was reading it would be back momentarily.

Kirk waited until everyone had gotten a good look around before resuming the story. "Once consummated, even against her will, the marriage was considered legal by both church and state. Francesca was forced to accept her fate as Gianciotto's wife. Although hurt and angry with Paolo for betraying her, she continued to secretly love him."

What fools women are when they're in love, Ava thought ruefully. She knew from experience how devastating a lover's betrayal could be, yet how the love and longing went on, undiminished.

"As members of the same family, Francesca and Paolo were constantly thrown together," Kirk continued. He stood beneath the coat of arms emblazoned on the fireplace, which was the only reminder of the power of the Malatesta family in the room.

"The situation must have become intolerable for Paolo, because he accepted the post of Captain of the People for the city of Florence. But if seeing Francesca all the time without being able to tell her how much he loved her had been a torment—" Kirk paused and his eyes darkened as though he knew exactly what Paolo must have gone through "—not seeing her at all must have been unendurable. Three months later, Paolo resigned his post for 'personal reasons' and returned here to the castle." A smile flickered like the candlelight over his face. "No longer able to deny their feelings for each other, Paolo and Francesca became lovers."

"What a simply fabulous story," exclaimed the English reporter, her notebook forgotten. "What happened next?"

"Rumors of their love affair reached Gianciotto. To trap them, he left the castle, pretending to go on a trip. He was sure the lovers couldn't resist the opportunity to be together." With slow, deliberate steps, Kirk walked over to the canopied bed.

Ava found herself watching Kirk as intently as the rest of the group. It occurred to her that he would have made a first-rate actor. His strong, dramatic features and towering physique, the undeniable power of his personality, gave him a natural stage presence. His deep, rough voice commanded attention. Like all great actors, he made it impossible for the audience to watch anything but him.

Kirk halted in front of the bed. "Paolo and Francesca were asleep in each other's arms," he resumed, his hushed tone almost evoking the lovers' presence in the canopied bed. "Suddenly Gianciotto banged on the locked door, demanding to be let in. Covering herself with her robe, Francesca went to open the door. Paolo only had time to throw his cloak around him to make good his escape."

With one lithe, swift motion, Kirk was in the center of the room. Bending over, he grabbed the iron ring embedded in the oak floor. Everyone gasped with surprise as he pulled open a rectangular panel in the floor. "This is the trapdoor Paolo used to visit Francesca." The top steps of a winding stairway hacked out of stone were visible through the opening; the rest of the stairs plunged into the darkness below.

"Assuming that her lover had gotten away safely, Francesca unbolted the door, letting her husband in. But Paolo's cloak had gotten caught in the trapdoor. Before he could free himself, Gianciotto saw him. Blind with rage, he pulled out his sword and rushed to attack his brother. In a desperate attempt to stop him, Francesca threw herself in front of Paolo and the sword went through her, also, killing them both."

"Why, it's like something out of Shakespeare," murmured the English reporter.

"Dante," Kirk corrected, letting the trapdoor fall closed. "The great Italian poet immortalized the lovers in his *Divine Comedy*."

"I heard about that," Lorraine Landis sniffed presumptuously. "Isn't that the book about all the different circles of hell?"

Kirk nodded in agreement. "Nine circles. Each one designed to punish a particular kind of sin." A wicked look gleamed in his eyes. "There's even a circle reserved for people who spread gossip and scandal. Their punishment is to be torn limb from limb."

"I don't believe in hell," Lorraine tossed back archly.

"But what if you're wrong?" Kirk relished the appalled look on the gossip queen's face almost as much as the delighted laugh Ava had been unable to suppress. It was the first time she had laughed all evening.

"That's the end of the tour, ladies and gentlemen," he announced, reaching for the candelabra. "I'm sure you all want to get back to the festivities. I know I do. Ava?" He offered her his arm and was pleased by how eagerly she took it.

She laughed again as he was leading her back down the hallway several long strides ahead of the others. "I don't think I'll ever forget the look on that woman's face when you told her there's a place waiting for her in hell." Admiration glowed in Ava's green eyes as she looked up at him, snagging something inside him.

"With all the harm she's done, that's just where she belongs."

"In which circle of hell did Dante put Paolo and Francesca?" Her tone made it clear that she felt they didn't deserve to be in hell at all.

"In the second circle, which is reserved for those who have sinned for love." The way she looked at that moment, her face alive with curiosity, her lips parted, soft and sensuous, he would gladly have gone to hell because of her. "Their punishment was to be tossed about by a fierce wind with only one another's body to cling to. They float in space like that, wrapped in each other's arms, for all eternity."

The light that flared in her eyes rivaled the glow of the candles. "Wrapped in each other's arms, for all eternity?"

"Hardly seems like hell, does it?" Kirk murmured wryly.

"No," Ava breathed. "That's *my* idea of heaven."

The longing in her voice, suffusing her exquisite face, made Kirk's blood jump. His eyes locked with hers. "I see we have the same idea of heaven."

Ava was too thrown to respond, nor was she able to break the connection between them. She remembered how his arms had felt wrapped around her, how she'd clung to him as though the world had dissolved around them. And how a mere kiss had seemed like a piece of eternity.

Kirk's pulse quickened as he read everything Ava was feeling in her wide, expressive eyes. His arm slid around her, pulling her close to him. "Let's get out of here."

"What?" Ava stammered, though the naked hunger on his face left no doubt as to why he wanted to leave. "But we can't just walk out in the middle of the reception. What about all those people?"

He laughed. "As Dante would say, to hell with them."

Ava swallowed convulsively. "But shouldn't we wait just a little longer?"

"No." His arm tightened around her possessively. "I'm not going to wait a moment longer. I've waited long enough."

Four

"Your bedroom is in here," Kirk said, throwing the paneled oak door open.

Ava stared at him uncomprehendingly for a moment. "*My* bedroom?"

"Yes." As much as he wanted to be with her, Kirk's pride wouldn't permit him to force his presence on Ava knowing how she felt about him. He was hoping that in time she would want to be with him, but the offer had to come from her. "I thought you'd feel more comfortable having a room of your own."

"Yes, I would," she admitted. "Thank you."

Though he knew it was foolish to hope that she'd be disappointed at not sharing his bed all night, her obvious relief hurt him more than he'd have thought possible.

"But where will you sleep?"

"My bedroom is directly across the hall from yours." With a wave of his hand, he indicated an identical door, also framed by a marble lintel. A long, awkward pause hung between them.

It was all Kirk could do not to grab Ava and haul her into his arms. He longed to sweep her off her feet and carry her over the threshold as a bridegroom should, to throw her down on the bed and make love to her until she wanted him as desperately as he wanted her.

He had to remind himself that she didn't feel the same way about him.

"I'll let you get ready, then," he managed politely. Turning abruptly, he entered his room before he did something he was afraid might ruin what little chance he had with her.

Ava jumped at the sound the door made when Kirk shut it behind him. She hadn't realized her nerves were so raw. Her hand was shaking when she closed the door to her room.

Despite the state she was in, Ava couldn't help but admire the lush Renaissance decor of the spacious bedroom with its travertine marble floor. A border of veined black marble made a gleaming contrast with the unique transparency of the white. High walls were veiled in white silk, and gold-tassled cords held the transparent drapes open midway, revealing richly detailed frescoes of prancing unicorns and other mythical beasts.

Yards of the same white silk, suspended from a gilded crown on the ceiling, cascaded in soft waves over the bed, while braided cords caught and held the billowing folds to the ivory-inlaid bedposts. The bedspread was of antique lace, and lace ruffles edged the sheets and pillows. The room appeared open to the heavens, an illusion created by the midnight-blue ceiling studded with gold stars that seemed to flicker in the firelight.

Her two beat-up suitcases, which Kirk had obviously had sent over from the hotel, looked as decidedly out of place amid such luxury as Ava felt. Continuing her inspection, she was surprised to discover that her clothes were already hanging in the inlaid armoire, her shoes lined up in a neat little row beneath them. In precise little piles, her lingerie lay folded inside the matching chest of drawers.

A bottle of champagne was chilling in a silver bucket on one of the night tables, and the fire crackling in the fireplace lent a soft warm glow to the room. The air was perfumed by masses of long-stemmed white roses that overflowed from several vases. The bed covers had even been turned down.

As usual, Kirk had taken care of everything, Ava noted resentfully, right down to the pink satin nightgown—part of the trousseau he'd insisted on buying for her—that was draped over the foot of the bed, waiting for her. She felt like just another object in that room, bought and paid for by Kirk Falconer, a possession to be enjoyed by him like the vintage champagne.

The bedroom suddenly felt so close she could barely breathe, the scent of roses almost unbearably sweet. Leaving behind the nightgown he was expecting her to wear, Ava went over to the door that opened onto a balcony. She pulled it open and stepped outside.

A bracing gust of wind whipped her long hair around her and sent the layers of her chiffon skirt swirling about her knees. The wind carried the murmur of the Adriatic up the steep hill, mingling the sea's salty tang with the refreshing scent of pine. Moonlight shimmered on the still waters and bathed the gnarled trees clinging to the jagged cliffs with an unreal glow.

"It's a lovely view, isn't it?" Kirk's voice came unexpectedly from behind, making her jump.

She spun around to face him, and her breath caught in her throat. He'd changed into a black robe in the style of a Japanese kimono. The simple but dramatic lines emphasized the powerful muscles of his shoulders and chest. Through the deep slash of the neckline curled the beginning of a thick mat of black hair. Coarse, dark hair covered his bare calves. She realized with a shock that he was naked under his robe.

"I didn't mean to startle you," he said, coming over to her. "I knocked several times. I guess you didn't hear me out here."

"No, I didn't."

Kirk was aware of the strain in Ava's voice, and he noticed that she hadn't changed into her nightgown. "Do you like your room?"

"How could anyone not like it?" she murmured politely but evasively.

"But do *you* like it?" he persisted. It meant a great deal to him.

"It's the most beautiful bedroom I've ever seen," Ava was forced to admit.

"If there's anything you want or need, anything at all, just let me know." Moonlight turned his steel-gray hair to silver and softened the harsh lines of his face. His mouth had never looked more inviting.

Turning away, Ava glanced down at the sea. "Everything's perfect the way it is. As usual, you've thought of absolutely everything."

The wry bitterness in her tone confused him. Any other woman, he knew, would have been dazzled by such luxury. He had to remind himself that she wasn't like the kind of women he was accustomed to—that was why he loved her. But it also made it damn near impossible for him to know how to treat her sometimes. Nothing he did seemed to work with her. He wanted her so much it hurt.

No matter how hard she fought it, Kirk's presence tugged at Ava's senses as inexorably as the moon pulled at the tide below. The silence that hung between them was electric, charged by the memory of the kiss they'd shared earlier, and the anticipation of the wedding night to come. Unable to stand the unnerving silence any longer, she said, "It really is lovely here."

"I was hoping you'd like it." His voice was deep and low, disturbingly intimate. "But I think we should go back inside. It's getting a bit chilly out here, don't you think?"

She took a step back, looking up at him with wide, fearful eyes. "I'm not chilly."

A wry smile flickered across his face as his dark gaze moved over her body. "You're trembling."

"Am I?" she lied defensively. "I wasn't aware of it."

"I am." The look he gave her told her that he knew the reason she was trembling had nothing to do with the wind or the fine mist suffusing the air. "It's time to go inside, Ava."

Before she could protest, he put his arm around her waist and led her back into the bedroom, closing the door behind them. Though he was holding her lightly, she could feel the power coiling the muscles of his arm, the warmth where his fingers curved around her waist. She knew he could feel how much she was shaking.

"I guess it was colder out there than I realized," she said, trying to explain away the reason for her nervousness.

"Here, sit by the fire." He released her beside the chaise lounge in front of the fireplace.

Ava sat down on the chaise sideways, choosing not to recline on it. Though welcome, the warmth of the fire was unable to penetrate the chill that was spreading through her from somewhere deep inside.

"Would you like some champagne?" Kirk asked graciously, already on his way over to the night table.

"Yes, I would," she got out with difficulty. "Thanks."

"It's Spumante, actually." Sliding the bottle out of the silver bucket, he wrapped a linen napkin around its neck. "Italian champagne. Have you ever tried it?"

"No."

"It's not as dry as French champagne." Swiftly he peeled off the gold foil and pulled off the tiny wire cage securing the cork. "It has a sweeter, more mellow taste. I think you'll like it."

Ava realized that Kirk was talking in an effort to get her to relax. She had the feeling that he was determined to be patient with her, and that patience didn't come easily to him. She watched as the cork slowly gave way under the expert pressure of his fingers. She couldn't imagine anything not giving way under his strong, supple hands. The loud pop made her jump once again.

"I believe a toast is in order," he murmured when he sat down on the edge of the chaise next to her and handed her a glass. His eyes met hers over the rim of his fluted glass. "To a love as deep and enduring as Paolo and Francesca's."

For a moment Ava thought he was joking. The hunger burning in his eyes assured her that he'd meant every word. Quickly she gulped down almost half of the sparkling wine.

"This really is delicious," she said, trying to ignore the dark intensity of his gaze, his disturbing closeness. "It is sweeter than French champagne," she rattled on, "and has a fruitier taste."

He took a long, slow swallow, his eyes never leaving hers. "It tastes almost as sweet as you do."

Ava's lips parted in surprise. She remembered how thoroughly his tongue had explored her mouth. She lowered her eyes, and saw that the way he was sitting, his robe hung open in front. Firelight flickered over the sleek, hard muscles of his chest, picking out the silvery curls among the thick, black ones.

Kirk smiled when he caught her staring. "You don't think I'm underdressed do you?"

Ava gulped down the rest of her wine.

"Or are you the one who's overdressed?" Humor glowed in his eyes as they moved over her chiffon dress, and he leaned toward her. "Did you need help with the zipper? Or didn't I give you enough time?"

"Yes...uh, no!" She set her glass down on the small marble table next to the chaise. "Kirk, I'm sorry, but I *am* going to need more time."

The teasing warmth went out of his eyes. He stared at her for a long moment. "How much more?" he asked evenly. He'd clearly understood that she hadn't been referring to changing her clothes. "A day? A week? A month? A year?"

"Just until we get to know each other."

He smiled crookedly. "I can't think of a better way for a man and woman to get to know each other than making love."

"That's just it," Ava cried, jumping to her feet. "We wouldn't be making love!"

"Oh, yes, we would!" With one lithe motion he was on his feet. "That's a promise." He took a step toward her.

Ava stepped back. "Kirk, please, you—"

"Ava, this isn't a part you're playing now that a few more weeks' rehearsals will make right," he broke in. "You're my wife. I want you to be my wife in every sense of the word."

"But I can't ... I never could be! I tried to tell you that earlier, but you wouldn't listen!" She saw pain flash in his eyes and tighten the rugged lines of his face. Regretting her harsh words, she put her hand on his arm. "It's not just with you, Kirk," she added softly, ruefully. "I can't love anyone."

"That's ridiculous," he said flat out, as though he knew her better than she knew herself.

"It's true," she cried brokenly.

He studied her intently for a moment. "Who is he, Ava?"

"What?"

"Who's the man who hurt you so deeply that you're afraid to let yourself love again?"

Ava stared at Kirk in amazement. She never would have expected him to be so perceptive. Though it still hurt her to talk about Derek, she realized that she owed Kirk an explanation. Slowly she sank down on the chaise lounge. "He was an actor I met five years ago. We belonged to the same acting class. He was the first man I ever..." Her voice trailed off.

"He was your first lover?" Kirk prompted, his voice tight.

"My first," she admitted haltingly, "and my only lover."

It was Kirk's turn to be amazed. He'd assumed that a woman as beautiful as Ava had had several lovers before she'd met him. Now he almost wished she had. She'd obviously loved that one man so deeply she'd been unable to forget him—maybe she still loved him.

"Tell me about him," he demanded, though part of him wasn't sure he really wanted to know.

"He was the most popular actor in class," she began reluctantly, turning her face toward the fire. "Everyone always said he'd be a star one day. He had everything it takes to be a great classical actor—looks, talent, charisma. All the girls in class were in love with him." She smiled self-consciously. "I had a crush on him for months, but I didn't think he even knew I was alive. Then one day, he asked me to do a scene with him, the balcony scene from *Romeo and Juliet*."

She drew in a long breath and let it out. "We were rehearsing the love scene one afternoon," she went on, staring into the fireplace as if she could see the experience unfolding in the blazing red-and-yellow flames. "And suddenly we weren't acting anymore. Our kisses were real. We forgot our lines, the scene. We forgot about everything."

Firelight flickered over Ava's rapt face, but it was the memory of her first love that made her eyes glow with an inner light, and it tore at Kirk.

The light went out of her eyes and she looked up at him as if she'd just remembered he was there. "And that's how we became lovers," she finished lamely.

"Was he in love with you, too?" Only with the greatest effort had Kirk been able to keep his tone totally devoid of emotion.

"He told me he was. I believed he was." She shook her head sadly. "That's why I can't understand how he could do what he did. We were both so happy those few months we had together." Her voice caught on what might have been a sob.

"What happened?" Kirk took a step closer to the chaise. "Why did it end?"

"It just...ended." Ava shrugged, trying to shake off the pain. "One day he got an offer to do a movie in Hollywood. He didn't even tell me about it." She laughed, but it came out in brittle, broken pieces. "He just left a message with my answering service."

"Jesus Christ!" Kirk muttered savagely. Knowing how sensitive Ava was, he had no trouble imagining how devastated she must have been. He understood why she'd shut herself off in a fantasy world ever since. Hope surged through him: she wasn't determined to resist him, but love itself.

He sat down on the chaise next to her. "Now I understand why you feel the way you do, Ava," he told her softly. "But you can't shut love out of your life forever because you've been hurt once, no matter how deeply."

"I'll leave love to those people who can take it lightly," she tossed back. "Since I can't, I'm better off without it."

He shook his head with a knowing smile. "No, you're not. You're much too emotional and sensuous a woman to deny yourself love."

His evaluation of her was so startling, Ava laughed in spite of herself. Derek had always teased her about how shy and insecure she was both as a woman and as a lover. "Where on earth did you get that idea about me?"

"I've seen those qualities in your acting," Kirk explained, "which is the only time you allow yourself to express your deepest feelings. I've watched you very closely on stage, Ava." His dark eyes met and held hers. "I've seen the longing for love you keep locked inside. I felt the sensuality you try so hard to deny when I kissed you earlier."

The image of herself that Ava saw reflected in Kirk's eyes left her too stunned to reply.

"Would you like me to prove it to you?" He slid close to her, so close she could feel the heat radiating from his body. "Kiss me," he ordered, bringing his face down to hers.

Ava's mouth went dry. Her throat felt so constricted all she could do was shake her head.

"You can make a liar out of me with just one kiss," he murmured wryly, his warm breath brushing her face.

"Kirk, please!" Her hands came up to splay across his chest. She felt powerful muscles clench at her touch. "Just give me a little more time and—"

"No," he said, his tone final. "I told you earlier, I've waited for you long enough." Reaching out unexpectedly, he slid both hands in her hair. "But I would have been willing to wait even longer if you hadn't responded to my kiss the way you did." Slowly, inexorably, he drew her face to within a breath of his. "You can't deny what happened between us, Ava. I won't let you deny it."

"Kirk, don't." Ava fought to twist free of him, but he was too strong for her. "You promised you wouldn't force yourself on me."

He laughed. "Feel free to stop me anytime you want," he murmured just before his mouth took hers.

Ava wasn't prepared for the aching tenderness of his kiss, so she had no defense against it. It touched something deep inside her, a longing for love she hadn't known was there. His mouth was unbelievably soft and warm. With deep, slow strokes, his tongue parted her lips, slipping inside before she realized what she was allowing to happen.

He made a sound in his throat when he tasted her, and his kiss became more intense, his tongue more daring, as it penetrated the deepest recesses of her mouth with an intimacy that left her helpless. She could do nothing to stop him or the shimmering waves of pleasure breaking over her.

"You're so sweet," he groaned against her mouth. "I never knew anything could taste so sweet." As if he were licking honey off a spoon, he ran his tongue from one corner of her lips to the other. Ava gasped and an uncontrollable shudder went through her. The hands she'd pressed to his chest before to push him away clenched, grabbing fistfuls of material warm with his body heat. With gentle strokes he slid his tongue over her mouth again. "God, I'd love to taste every inch of you."

Fear shivered through her at his words, at the hunger she saw coiling in the depths of his eyes. She tried to twist free of him, but his hands tightened in her hair.

"Don't be afraid of me," he pleaded, his voice raw.

"I'm not afraid of you." She had to lower her face so he wouldn't see the lie in her eyes.

"Yes, you are," Kirk murmured ruefully, his hands sliding out of her hair. With one finger he lifted her chin, bringing her eyes back to his. "You are afraid of me. But it's not for the reason you think." Bending his head, he brushed her lips softly, sensuously with his, and drank in the tiny whimper that escaped her. "I felt it after I kissed you the first time, but I couldn't understand why you were so afraid...until now." He smiled. "A woman like you could never have responded the way you did unless you felt something for me."

"No!" Pushing away from him, Ava jumped up from the chaise. "No, I don't! I don't know why that happened. It must have been seeing the castle for the first time in the moonlight or I just got caught up in the fantasy of—"

"No more fantasies!" he interrupted impatiently. "You won't need them with me." With one powerful motion he sprang to his feet and grabbed her wrist as she was about to walk away, pulling her up against him. "I've got something better for you!" Powerful arms locked around her and his mouth came down hard on hers. There was no tenderness in his kiss now, as he strove to wipe everything out of her consciousness but the undeniable realities of his bruising mouth and vibrant body.

Unable to defend herself against his superior strength, Ava tried to resist his erotic assault on her senses. But his mouth moved on hers with a hunger that was more than just physical, unleashing a responding hunger in her that was just as frightening in its intensity. In a mindless daze, she wondered how he could have such an effect on her when she didn't love him. Her arms went up to circle his neck and her trembling lips opened to the deep, possessive thrust of his tongue.

A groan of pure male satisfaction tore out of Kirk when he felt all resistance go out of her and she melted in his arms. Desire surged through him, hot and hard, just barely within his control. "If you're going to stop me," he muttered raggedly, "you better stop me now."

Ava's eyes fluttered open, dazed with sensations she'd only dreamed of, and though she tried to speak, she couldn't. When she saw the look of triumph that flashed in Kirk's eyes she regretted her moment of indecision, but by then his mouth had closed over hers again, taking away her breath, along with her last shred of reason.

The hunger for her that had been eating away at him from the first day he'd met Ava raged through Kirk, making it impossible for him to go as slowly with her as he'd promised himself he would. With hard, deep thrusts of his tongue he filled her mouth the way he ached to fill her body. Her breasts shuddered against his chest and she gave herself up to him unhesitatingly.

Swiftly his hands moved to find the zipper on her dress and remove the last barrier between them. As he was fumbling the zipper open, it caught on a piece of fabric and jammed. He could feel her body heating under his, every soft curve melting with longing against him. He ripped the zipper open.

Ava gasped and pulled her mouth away. Fear shivered through her at the sound the chiffon made as it came apart in his hands. She was so open to him now, utterly defenseless, as easy to destroy as the delicate fabric he was shredding so carelessly. Her arms slid from around his neck and she stepped back, but that only made it easier for him to strip the dress off her. Piece by piece he tore off her lacy underwear, too quickly for her to stop him, and tossed them aside impatiently.

Only when she stood before him as in his fantasies, with her luxuriant hair cascading down her naked body, did Kirk notice that Ava was shaking uncontrollably. He could see that she felt her nakedness to be more than skin-deep. Her vulnerability brought a feeling of tenderness such as he'd never known for any woman welling up inside him.

"I'm sorry I was so rough," he apologized thickly, "but if you only knew how much I've wanted this."

Pulling the front of his robe open, he wrapped it around her trembling body, his arms holding it closed at her back as he drew her up against him. Ava gasped at the feel of his heated skin on hers, the unexpected intimacy of sharing his robe.

"I've wanted you from the moment I saw you," he grated, his breath warm and unsteady in her hair, the heat from his body melting through to her bones, dissolving the last paralyzing shred of fear. The robe was like a cocoon around her, binding her softly to him, blocking out all sensations beyond him. His mouth slid down to the pulse beating erratically at the base of her throat. "I've never been so hungry for anyone in my life."

Cool air suddenly shivered down Ava's back as the robe fell open, and Kirk's hands slid down to her hips to pull them tightly against his. Her breath caught when she felt him, rigid with desire, pressing against her tender flesh. Heat flowed from deep inside her with a melting rush.

Kirk felt her open to him, unfolding like the petals of a flower, all dewy, satin smooth, and it almost drove him beyond control. Fiercely his hands gripped her rounded bottom. His eyes gleamed feverishly in the firelight, while skin sliding on skin, he lifted her until her breasts hung poised over his mouth.

Ava cried out when she felt his mouth on her, hot and ravenous. She grabbed on to his shoulders, her nails sinking through fabric to the tightly coiled muscles beneath. His lips and teeth never stopped tugging at her, splintering her with pleasure, while he carried her over to the bed.

Nor did he release her when he sank down onto the bed with her, taking only a moment to shrug out of his robe. His hands swallowed up her breasts, pressing them together so his mouth could move easily between them. With stinging bites he tormented her nipples into swollen aching peaks, then soothed them with long, wet strokes of his tongue.

Mindlessly Ava buried her hands in Kirk's hair, as she arched her breasts against him, wanting him to take more of her, all of her.

He laughed in triumph that he could bring her to this wildness she'd never been capable of, a raw hunger she was powerless to deny. Part of her hated him for reveling in the power he had over her body, but that didn't stop the need for him that went as deep as the emptiness inside her, an emptiness only he could fill.

He slid down her body, his hands rushing ahead to part her thighs, only to wrap them around him. She stiffened in shock as his heated breath caressed her—never had she been touched so intimately. When he sought to open her with burning kisses, a strangled protest tore out of her.

Lifting his head, he glanced at her. "I told you I want everything you have to give," he said. "I want all of you." His hands slid under her hips. "And I'm not going to stop until I get what I want." Slowly, deliberately, he lifted her hips to meet his descending mouth.

All the love Kirk felt for Ava, a love he knew she didn't want, surged through him, melting into his blood. Making her his in a way he never had any woman, he poured his love over her until she was twisting wildly beneath him and he felt the burning, quivering spasms as desire took her, giving her wholly, finally to him. Swiftly he moved up her body and buried himself inside her.

Ava cried out when she felt the full extent of his possession, a possession that was more than physical, that demanded an equal response from her. He filled all of her, yet he thrust even deeper, seeking and wanting more. With each powerful thrust she felt herself opening to him, until he was so deep inside her, so much a part of her, she didn't know where she ended and he began.

A fire storm of passion broke over them, shaking them. With only each other's body to cling to, the world dissolved around them and a single moment became eternity. All the fires of hell couldn't have burned hotter or with such delicious torment, fusing them together. As one they were consumed in the same burning, convulsive explosion.

Five

In her sleep Ava reached out, seeking the resilient warmth of Kirk's body. Finding only emptiness, she awoke. The pale, tentative beginnings of dawn filtered through the windows, illuminating the empty space beside her. A quick search of the bedroom confirmed what she had somehow sensed in her sleep: he was gone.

She wondered when he'd left. When she remembered how he'd clung to her in the aftermath of passion as though he never wanted to let her go, she wondered why. She was surprised to find that she missed the feel of his arm around her, his hand cupping her breast possessively even in sleep, the hair-roughened thigh he'd slung over her hip.

Frame by frame, everything that had happened between them unreeled in her mind like an indelible film. Heat flamed in her cheeks and flowed from deep inside her. She was amazed she'd once thought him cold and passionless. In recalling the tender way he'd wrapped his robe around her when he saw how frightened she was at first, strange new feelings stirred within her.

The sight of a colorfully wrapped box propped up against the base of the wine cooler on the night table caught her attention. She didn't remember it being there last night. Looking closer, she noticed a card tucked inside the satin ribbon. It read simply: "To Ava, from Kirk."

Picking up the long, slender package, she unwrapped it, uncovering a black velvet box. She drew in a shocked breath when she snapped the box open, revealing an emerald pendant suspended by a cluster of diamonds from a platinum chain. Even in the half-light the exquisitely cut facets of the huge emerald caught and refracted the light, gleaming as though a blue flame burned in its depths.

The pendant had to have cost thousands of dollars, yet Ava had never felt so cheap. Kirk Falconer always got what he wanted because he was willing to pay the price, she reminded herself bitterly; he'd told her so himself. Last night he finally got what he wanted from her, and now he was paying her for it.

Ava snapped the box shut and slammed it down on the night table. The warm feeling she'd felt momentarily for Kirk disintegrated, replaced by a cold rage. How could she have ever believed she'd been wrong about him? How could she have opened herself to him as she had last night, as she never had before, not even to Derek?

It would never happen again, she promised herself.

Tears burned behind her eyes. She hadn't realized how much last night had meant to her until he'd destroyed it.

Falling back against the pillows, Ava forced all thoughts of Kirk out of her mind. But no matter how she tossed and turned she couldn't get comfortable again. The fire had gone out. Only ashes remained in the fireplace, as gray as the light filtering through the sheer drapes, as cold as the chill permeating the room. With blank eyes she stared up at the ceiling. In the growing daylight the ceiling was revealed for what it was: a painted sky with flat lifeless stars.

Ava was already out of bed when she got her wake-up call at seven. She'd showered and had just finished blow-drying her hair, when she heard a knock on her door. Expecting Kirk, she came to a tense halt and pulled her robe closed tightly around her.

"*Permesso, signora?*" a robust, handsome woman in her late forties asked politely as she let herself in, carrying a continental breakfast on a large silver tray. She wore a simple, almost severe black dress, and her thick, dark hair was pulled into a neat bun at her nape. Her strong-boned features were softened by a wide, generous mouth and warm eyes.

She stopped as though surprised when she saw Ava standing in the middle of the room and glanced questioningly at the empty bed. "The *signora* is not having breakfast in bed?" she inquired with just the trace of an accent.

Ava had never had breakfast in bed in her life. "No."

The woman frowned slightly at her answer. "On the *balcone*, then?"

"Is that the balcony?" Ava asked, feeling ignorant and out of place. She knew she didn't belong in such surroundings, and she was sure the woman knew it, too. "No, thanks."

"Oh, *capisco*," she said, brightening. "The *signora* prefers to have breakfast with Signor Kirk. The *signore* has ordered a big American breakfast and he has asked if you would join him."

"No," Ava returned with more force than she'd intended, then quickly added, "I never eat a big breakfast."

"This is what I myself said to Signor Kirk. A *signora* never eats a big breakfast." She shifted her weight to her other foot, resting the tray against her middle. "Where would the *signora* care to eat?"

Ava was unaccustomed to giving orders and it bothered her that she was keeping the poor woman standing there, holding such an enormous tray. "Please, just put the tray down...anywhere."

"Va bene, signora." With brisk steps, she carried the tray over to the marble table set into a glass-enclosed alcove with a sweeping view of the sea. "I am Marina," she introduced herself with a warm smile. "I will be taking care of running the house for the *signora* for as long as she is here."

With perfect balance, she lifted two silver carafes in either hand and poured two hot even streams, one of coffee and one of milk, into the largest coffee cup Ava had ever seen. *"Caffelatte,"* she explained when she saw the curious look on Ava's face. "This is what we Italians drink at breakfast. But if the *signora* would prefer American coffee...or tea perhaps?"

"No, that's fine," Ava assured her, walking over to the alcove. "Please, don't bother," she hastened to add as the housekeeper was pulling one of the elaborately carved chairs away from the table so Ava could sit down. "I'll just have the *caffelatte*, thanks."

The woman looked down at the freshly baked rolls and croissants, the curls of softened butter and pots of jam, as if to make sure she'd prepared everything properly. "Just *caffelatte*?" She sounded terribly disappointed.

Ava felt awful. "I'm not hungry," she explained apologetically.

With a soft, indulgent laugh, Marina pushed the chair back in place. "Ah, when one is young and a new bride like the *signora*, one is only hungry for love."

Heat flowed under Ava's skin as memories of her wedding night washed over her. Grabbing the large coffee cup in both hands, she raised it to her lips.

"*Buono?*" Marina asked after Ava had downed a gulp of the strong, yet mellow brew. "The *caffelatte*, it is good?"

"Very... *buono*," Ava assured her sincerely.

The housekeeper's eyes lit up with pleasure, making Ava realize how much pride she took in pleasing others. "Does the *signora* require anything else?"

"No, Marina, thanks. And please, don't call me '*signora*.' My name is Ava."

"Signora Ava?"

"No, just Ava."

"Ah, I see you are just like Signor Kirk," she said, appraising Ava with dark, knowing eyes. "Very democratic, very American. I will enjoy working for you." In her strong, brisk manner, she started for the door. "Now I must see to Signor Kirk's breakfast." Just before she closed the door behind her, she sent Ava a soft smile. "May I say I wish you and Signor Kirk much love and happiness."

Ava was touched by Marina's wish, even though she knew there was little chance of it coming true. That saddened her somehow. She had to remind herself that she hadn't married Kirk for love or happiness, nor were those the reasons he'd married her. From across the room she glared at the black velvet box on the night table. At least now she knew what he wanted from her. She wanted nothing from him.

On her way over to the armoire, she paused to pick up her chiffon dress and lacy underwear, which were still scattered about the floor. Something tightened inside her when she remembered how he'd practically torn them off her. With an exasperated curse, she dropped the garments on the chaise lounge and continued over to the armoire.

Quickly she threw on a light sweater and a pair of jeans. She was determined to get downstairs before Kirk finished his breakfast and came looking for her. Pausing only to check her oversize bag to make sure her script was inside, she rushed out the door.

She deliberately left the emerald pendant behind.

"Signor Kirk, I have searched in all the rooms for the *signora*," Marina said, coming to a halt in front of the dining table, "and she is not to be found."

With a perplexed frown, Kirk pushed his empty plate aside and reached for his coffee. "She must be somewhere, Marina. Didn't you tell her I wanted her to join me for breakfast?"

"*Certo*, but she says she does not eat a big breakfast." She lifted her strong shoulders as if to say, "I told you so." "She did not even eat the rolls or croissants I brought her. *Niente*, just *caffelatte*."

"I see." Trying to hide his disappointment, Kirk took a slow sip of coffee. "Well, as you know, today's our first day of shooting. I'm sure she has a lot of things to take care of."

"Perhaps. But where?" With expressive hands, she punctuated her words. "She is not in her room."

"Do me a favor, go and check again, will you, Marina? She's not familiar with the villa and she may have gotten lost."

"*Va bene*," Marina agreed with a resigned sigh.

Kirk took a long, thoughtful swallow of coffee. More than ever, he regretted not having stayed with Ava all night as he'd wanted to. They would be having breakfast in bed now, or, better still, they wouldn't be having breakfast at all—just each other. Heat surged through him as he remembered how she'd felt in his arms. Leaving her soft, warm body to go back to his empty bed had been one of the most difficult things he'd ever had to do.

He wished he hadn't promised to respect her privacy, but he couldn't go back on his word their very first night together. He knew it would take time before she accepted him as her husband in the deepest sense of the word, and then *she* would be the one who wanted him to stay. After her response to him last night, he was sure that wouldn't take as long as he'd feared. Not even in his wildest fantasies had she given herself to him so completely. No woman ever had.

Setting his empty coffee cup down, Kirk smiled to himself. He wondered what Ava's reaction had been to the present he'd left her in his place.

"Signor Kirk, the *signora* is *assolutamente* not in her room," Marina announced when she came striding purposefully into the dining room a few minutes later. "And in her haste to get ready, she has left this behind." Carefully she set the velvet box down on the table in front of Kirk. "I did not think such a thing should be left lying about."

Reaching for the box, Kirk snapped it open. The emerald pendant had not even been removed from the metal pins securing it to the satin cushion. "Thanks, Marina."

"Shall I put it in the safe?"

"No, I'll keep it for her." Snapping the box shut, he slid it into his inside jacket pocket. He could no longer suppress the feeling that something was wrong. "So you still haven't found her?"

"No. The *signora* is not in any of the rooms. I have—"

"That is because she is in the garden, Marina," Marco interrupted as he came sauntering in. "I have seen her myself just some moments ago."

A wave of relief swept over Kirk. "What's she doing out there?" he asked, getting to his feet.

"That I am unable to know," the chauffeur said. "Maybe she is...how you say?" He knitted his thick brows while he searched for the correct word. "Desirous to make the movies."

Kirk couldn't help smiling at Marco's unique choice of words.

"'Desirous'—that is not correct?" the young man asked, looking over at Marina for confirmation.

"No. 'Impatient' is what you mean," Marina told him as she began collecting the breakfast dishes. "'Desirous' is correct when you talk of wanting to make love."

"Ah, love," sighed Marco.

"Come on, Marco," Kirk ordered, smiling. "It's getting late, and we're all desirous to make the movies."

"Si, signore!" But Marco continued leering, playfully at Marina.

Marina grumbled something about Casanova, as she set the dishes down on the tray.

Marco laughed as he hurried to join Kirk. "Is it my fault that I love women?"

"Your fault is that you love *all* women," Marina called after him.

"How can a man not love all women?" Marco appealed to Kirk, following him out the door. "Young, old, tall, short, fat, skinny. Each in her own way, they are all beautiful. And I love them all."

"Yes, I noticed," Kirk murmured wryly. "But haven't you ever loved just one woman?"

"*Certo!*" Marco exclaimed proudly. "Many times."

Kirk smiled crookedly at the young man's cavalier attitude toward love. It was an attitude he recognized. Though he'd never been a womanizer like Marco, until he'd met Ava he'd never felt the need to commit himself emotionally.

"One of these days, Marco," he predicted while they crossed the marble-walled foyer, "you're going to meet a very special lady, and then you won't be able to so much as look at another woman."

"Such a thing is not possible, I think, Signor Kirk," Marco protested. Moving quickly ahead of his boss, he pulled the front door open and held it for him. "One woman cannot satisfy all of a man's desires."

"She can if she's the right woman," Kirk found himself admitting. But two months ago he wouldn't have believed that was possible, either. From where he was standing, the limousine Marco had left idling in the driveway was fully visible. Ava was sitting in the back seat. The mere sight of her held Kirk transfixed in the doorway and sent his blood pulsing through him.

She was wearing her hair his favorite way, parted simply in the middle, cascading in thick, dark waves over her shoulders and back. She wore no makeup. She didn't need any. Her skin seemed to absorb the uniquely golden Italian light and reflect it back with a translucency no foundation could match. Without benefit of mascara, her eyelashes were a long, black fringe. Nor did she require any lipstick that morning. Still swollen from his kisses, her lips had never been redder or more unknowingly sensuous.

He was becoming aroused just remembering the feel of her soft, warm lips. The taste of her was still in his mouth.

Instead of diminishing his hunger, as he'd thought it would, making love to her had only made him hungry for more. He drew in a long, steadying breath and sighed it out. "Take it from me, Marco, the right woman can satisfy desires you didn't even know you had."

"So you, Signor Kirk, have found just such a woman." Following the line of Kirk's intense gaze, Marco looked over at Ava. She was too immersed in the script she was memorizing to realize that she was being watched. "Ah, Miss Kendall, she is *bellissima*."

Kirk heard the longing in Marco's tone. "She is also my wife," he reminded him flatly. "And don't you forget it."

"Never could I forget such a thing," Marco was quick to reassure him. "I like too much to live."

Kirk slanted him a bemused look as they stepped out on the veranda. "Why did you say that?"

"Because a man such as yourself would never let another man take his woman from him, this I am sure of," Marco replied with uncharacteristic seriousness. "I think you would kill such a man first."

"And I think you've seen too many operas, Marco," Kirk returned wryly.

But as they walked toward the limo, Kirk wondered what he'd do if Ava fell in love with someone else. Just the thought of her giving herself to another man as she had to him last night was enough to tear him up.

He honestly didn't know what he would do.

Through the open car window, Ava heard the sound of gravel crunching under the men's feet. She looked up from the script she'd been trying to concentrate on and watched Kirk's approach with a combination of resentment and fascination.

He was wearing a double-breasted, gray flannel suit that was only a shade lighter than his carefully groomed hair.

She'd never completely understood the term "power dressing," until that moment. The ease with which he wore his custom-made clothes, the sure, strong way he moved, everything about him exuded control and power. She found it difficult to believe he was the same man who'd made love to her with such overwhelming passion. She had no trouble believing he always paid for his pleasures.

"So, *here* you are," he said while Marco held the car door open for him. "I was about to send the bloodhounds out after you."

"I didn't know where you were, either," Ava returned pointedly. All she knew was that once he'd gotten what he'd wanted from her, he'd left her, and she wasn't about to go looking for him.

"I was in the dining room," he said, sliding easily onto the seat next to her. "Didn't Marina tell you I was having breakfast? I was hoping you'd join me."

"I never eat breakfast." Especially, she thought angrily, when instead of asking her himself he'd sent a servant with his orders. She went back to her script.

She could feel him studying her intently. In the tense silence that hung between them, the sound of the door being shut, the crunch of gravel as the chauffeur walked around to the other side of the car seemed louder than normal.

"*Buon giorno*, Miss Kendall," Marco said, after he'd slipped behind the wheel.

"*Buon giorno*, Marco," Ava returned with a tentative smile.

That was more than she'd given him, Kirk realized as Marco pulled out of the driveway and Ava buried herself in the script again. He hadn't expected such indifference from her after last night. He felt confused and hurt. He didn't know what to do. He did the only thing he knew.

Reaching into his pocket, he removed the velvet box and offered it to her. "It seems you forgot this."

Slowly she turned to face him. "No, I didn't forget it."

"I realize this doesn't go with blue jeans," he allowed wryly, snapping the box open to reveal the dazzling emerald pendant. "But would you mind trying it on? I'd like to see how it looks on you."

Ava shook her head. "I can't accept that, Kirk."

He smiled incredulously. He'd never known a woman to refuse an expensive gift before. "You can't accept a gift from your husband?"

"That's not a gift," Ava cried with all the pent-up hurt and resentment that were in her. "That's payment for services rendered!"

Kirk went very still, and the rugged lines of his face hardened. Bending forward, he slid the frosted glass partition closed and checked to make sure the chauffeur's attention was on the road. Then he turned back to her. "Services rendered?" he repeated, his voice savage. "Is that all you think last night meant to me?"

Ava was so thrown by the intensity of his reaction she couldn't answer.

"Or is that all it meant to you?" Snapping the box shut, he tossed it on top of the script in her lap. "You might as well take it, since you seem to feel you've earned it."

"That's exactly how you made me feel! You think you can buy anything, because money is all you really know or care about!" Proudly she tossed his gift back at him. "Well, you can't buy *me*!"

"I already have," he reminded her brutally.

Ava gasped as though he'd struck her; no slap could have hurt her more. "No, you haven't, and you never will," she got out with difficulty. "All you bought was the right to go to bed with me. But you can't buy love."

"Sure you can," Kirk said bitterly. "It just costs more." A sarcastic smile slashed his mouth. "Tell me, what *is* the going rate for love these days?"

"I'm not surprised *you* wouldn't know that," she said contemptuously. "Love can only be bought with love."

Sitting up abruptly, he leaned toward her. "You mean, all I have to do to get your love is admit that I love you?" His tone was as sardonic as before, but his eyes searched hers with an intensity she found confusing and deeply disturbing.

Ava dropped her eyes. "But we both know you don't love me."

"I'd be a damned fool if I did, wouldn't I?" he shot back. "Because you don't want anything I have to give, least of all my love!" With one savage swing of his arm, he threw the emerald pendant out the car window.

"Kirk, are you crazy?" Ava cried as the velvet box disappeared among a grove of cypress trees. "That pendant must have cost thousands of dollars!"

"That should give you some idea how much money means to me," he said caustically.

He didn't speak to her again until they were crossing the open courtyard of the castle to the shelter of the arcade, and then his tone was purely professional. "You remember where your dressing room is?"

"Yes, of course."

"Then you can start getting ready. I'm going to track down Hal to let him know we've arrived." Without hesitation, he left her standing in the middle of the arcade to go in search of the director.

Ava was grateful that she had so many things to do she couldn't afford to think about Kirk or the argument they'd had. By the time Makeup and Hair were through with her and she'd changed into her costume, all she could think about was the scene that was scheduled for that morning.

Yet when she went on to the set, anxiety churning up her stomach, she searched for Kirk among the bustling crowd of actors and crew, the tangle of lights and sound equipment. She was oddly disappointed to find that he wasn't there.

"Here's our Francesca now," Hal Dunhill, the director, called out as he started toward her in that easy, laid-back way of his. With deliberateness, he took in her medieval costume and hairdo. "Beautiful . . . just beautiful." He looked around thoughtfully. "Now where's Paolo *il bello*?"

"Right here, Hal," a deep, expressive voice said in back of Ava.

Ava's breath caught and the blood drained from her face when she turned around.

"Here's your Paolo, Francesca," Hal said easily. "I'm sure he doesn't need any introduction."

"I certainly hope not," Derek Granger said with a devastating smile.

Six

Cut!'' the director shouted, freezing Ava in the middle of her line, bringing everything to a standstill. He turned to the cameraman. "What happened this time?"

The cameraman threw his hands up. "She's out of frame. She missed her mark again."

"Francesca, you missed your mark again," Hal said, coming over to her with a leisurely gait, like a long distance runner pacing himself for the distance.

"I'm sorry," Ava apologized with a nervous glance at Kirk, who was watching the scene from the sidelines. It was the third time she'd missed her mark, and she'd forgotten her lines twice because she was so rattled over working with Derek. "I'm really sorry, I—"

"Not to worry. It's the first day and we're all a bit anxious," Hal told her with the soothing but weary smile of a seasoned professional. A twenty-year veteran of the Hollywood wars, nothing surprised, shocked, or could get a rise out of him. His features were as even and bland as his manner, and his voice sought only to calm and reassure.

"Barry?" he said over his shoulder to the first assistant director as he pointed to the mark on the floor. "Please put a bigger piece of tape down there. I think she's having trouble seeing it."

While the A.D. was carrying out his order, Hal drew Ava to one side. "I like what you're doing, Francesca. The work is good. I see the pain. I see you fighting the attraction. So just give me the same thing, but on the mark, okay?"

Ava nodded. "I'll get it this time."

"Good girl. Now, Paolo," He motioned for Derek to join them. "I like what you've got, so keep it. Just give me a little more guilt."

A perplexed frown creased Derek's perfectly chiseled features. "Guilt?"

"Even though you're trying to justify your betrayal to Francesca, you know how much you've hurt her," the director explained. "I want to see that." As he was walking back to his chair, he added, "By the way, the sexual tension between the two of you is right on the money. Let's keep it."

Derek smiled. "That's easy," he said under his breath to Ava as they were returning to their places. "That's not acting."

"It is on my part," she returned pointedly. But as she watched her ex-lover resume his starting position, Ava knew she was lying.

Derek had never looked more devastatingly attractive. His curly black hair was longer than she remembered, spilling over the fur-trimmed edge of his costume. The short medieval tunic and matching purple tights emphasized the long, elegant lines of his body. Years of dancing and fencing lessons infused his every movement with a supple grace. He had the longest eyelashes she'd ever seen on a man, and the thick black fringe heightened the startling blue of his eyes.

A feeling of deep, aching loss threatened to swamp Ava, but she told herself that Francesca must have felt the same way when she saw Paolo again. As she had for the past five years, Ava buried her real feelings in the part she was playing, knowing that was the only way they couldn't hurt her.

"Okay, everybody," Hal called out when he'd eased himself into the high director's chair. "Quiet on the set. We're going for another take."

"Quiet on the set!" the A.D. shouted, though everyone had hushed instantly.

"Roll sound. Roll camera," the director ordered. "Mark it."

The second A.D. held the clapboard up in front of the camera. "Scene twelve. Take six."

It required eight more takes before everything went perfectly and Hal finally announced, "That's a print. Actors take five while we set up for the reverse shot."

Ava let out a long sigh of relief.

"I enjoyed that," Derek told her with a charming grin. "It's been a long time since I enjoyed acting that much." His eyes locked with hers, while a world of memories gleamed in their brilliant depths. "We always did work beautifully together."

"Did we?" Ava forced a casual shrug. "I don't remember." She turned and walked away from him. Her legs were shaking. She felt so emotionally drained she didn't know how she'd be able to go through the scene with him again. While the grips began moving lights and equipment in order to reshoot the scene from the opposite angle, she made her way over to the sidelines, where Kirk was waiting for her.

"Are you all right, Ava?" Kirk asked, searching her face intently.

Ava was surprised that Kirk was aware of the state she was in. She wondered whether he'd also picked up on the sensual tension between herself and Derek. "Kirk, there's something I have to... could we go to my dressing room a minute?"

Before Kirk could reply, Ava's father came rushing over to them. "You were great, princess!" Mike exclaimed. "There are just a couple of very minor things I want to point out to you."

"Please, not now, Mike," Ava pleaded. "I just want to go to my dressing room and—"

"That's a great idea," Mike said, stepping out of the way to let the set dresser by. "I have a few suggestions on how you should play—"

"We already have a director on the set," Kirk cut him off, not bothering to hide his annoyance. "Aren't you supposed to be in Makeup, Mike?"

"I was just on my way, but I wanted to see how Ava was doing."

"Don't worry about Ava," Kirk said flatly. "Ava's doing just fine. You just worry about getting yourself into costume and makeup. Your scene's scheduled right after the next setup."

"Sure, I know. I'm ready...practically." He gave Ava's arm a quick squeeze. "I'll talk to you later, princess. You know where to find me if you need me." Catching the look Kirk shot him, he hurried off.

Kirk let out a sigh of exasperation. "Why do you always let your father do that to you?"

"Do what?" Ava murmured distractedly. Derek was standing across the way from them, staring at her intensely.

"What's wrong, Ava?"

"I can't talk here. There's so much confusion."

"Come on, let's go to your dressing room. They won't need you for at least half an hour." Kirk took Ava's arm and felt how tense she was through the silky fabric of her costume. "What are you upset about? You were wonderful. The scene played like a dream."

"But look at all the mistakes I made," she said miserably as he led her off the set. "I'm sorry, Kirk. I never had so much trouble getting through a scene in my life."

"What ends up on the screen is all that counts," Kirk assured her softly. Her vulnerability made him forget the hurt and anger he'd been carrying around since their argument in the car. "As Hal said, everyone's anxious the first day."

"It's not that, I..." Ava came to a halt at the top of the marble staircase leading to the courtyard. "Kirk, why didn't you tell me that Derek Granger was going to play Paolo?"

"Because I didn't know for sure that he would."

"But you're the producer," she protested, lifting the embroidered hem of her gown as they started down the stairs. "How's that possible?"

"It was touch and go right down to the last day as to whether Derek's shrink thought he was ready to handle it."

"What do you mean?"

"You read the papers." He stopped to pick up the train of her gown to make sure it wouldn't get tangled in her heels during their long descent. "I'm sure you're aware of the drinking problem Derek's been having these past few years."

For years after Derek had become famous, Ava had gone out of her way not to read anything about him, but she'd been unable to ignore the headlines proclaiming his drunken brawls, his well-publicized battles with his directors, or his stormy love affairs. "I didn't know his drinking had become a problem."

"It's practically destroyed his career." Kirk dropped the train of her gown once they'd cleared the staircase. "No one in Hollywood will hire him anymore."

Ava slid Kirk a long, questioning glance as they proceeded under the arcade to the star dressing rooms. "Then why did *you* hire him?"

"Because he's perfect for the part," he replied as if it were obvious. "I've never even considered anyone else. There isn't another American actor with his looks and talent who can handle classical roles the way he can."

It was impossible to argue with that. "But is he worth all the trouble?" Reaching out, she grabbed his arm. "Kirk, I'm sure he's going to make trouble for us."

"That's how the studio felt about him, too," Kirk admitted. "That's why I had to hire John Colby as a standby."

"Then why don't you use him instead?" Ava demanded.

Kirk laughed. "Are you serious?"

Her hand slid off his arm. "Very serious, Kirk."

The intensity in Ava's tone brought Kirk to a stop in front of the arched door to her dressing room. "You're asking me to replace a Derek Granger with a John Colby?"

"John Colby's a very good actor. He's proved himself in any number of Shakespearean plays."

"Yes," Kirk agreed, pushing the door to her dressing room open. "Colby's a good dependable actor who'll give me a good dependable performance. But I want an electrifying performance. Only Derek Granger can give me that."

"If you can get him to give the performance," Ava countered, sweeping past Kirk into the improvised dressing room.

"I will." He followed her inside with the same easy assurance. With a flick of his finger he located the artfully disguised light switch, and the circular iron chandelier hanging from a chain in the center of the vaulted ceiling came alive. Its many tiers of "candles" were made of waxed cardboard; electric light bulbs in the shape of flames sought to retain the illusion of another era.

The hand-carved reproductions of the medieval table and chairs had been removed since yesterday, replaced by a collapsible stainless steel table holding a three-way makeup mirror and an assortment of theatrical makeup and brushes. A full-length mirror stood in one corner of the room, reflecting the movable clothes rack that took up an entire wall and held Ava's costumes, each one tagged with the appropriate scene number. The wrought-iron daybed resting against the opposite wall and several portable chairs completed the new furnishings, making a strange contrast with the medieval architecture.

"I admit there's an element of risk with Derek," Kirk went on, "but I've never believed in playing it safe. I've always believed in taking a chance on people—special people." A wry smile tugged at the corners of his mouth as he halted in front of her. "I took a chance on you."

"On me?" Ava looked up at him uncomprehendingly.

"The studio wanted an established star for the part of Francesca. I wanted you. I had to fight long and hard to get you, but I did."

"But how?"

"I simply convinced them of the obvious. When this movie is released you *will* be a star." His tone brooked no argument, and his eyes, when they met hers, glowed with a faith as sure and compelling as his presence.

"And I think Derek deserves a chance, too," Kirk added. "He just got caught in the Hollywood trap like so many others. He became a star with his first movie and he couldn't handle all that success." He shook his head ruefully. "Too much, too soon. I've seen it wreck the best of them. They start drinking or doing drugs as an escape from the pressures and special problems success brings. Pretty soon the escape becomes the trap."

Ava turned away. "That's not the only reason I refuse to work with him."

"Ava, listen to me." Reaching out, Kirk took Ava by the shoulders and turned her back to him. "Derek hasn't had a drink in over four months, and he's promised me he'll never touch another drop. I'm going to see to it that he keeps that promise." He smiled reassuringly. "So don't you worry about Derek Granger. That's my job. I'll take care of him."

"But I'm the one who has to act with him," Ava protested with more emotion than she'd intended. "And I can't, Kirk, I just can't!"

"How can you say that after the scene you just did with him? You were both fantastic."

"It took me fourteen takes to get that scene right because I was having so much trouble working with him," she blurted out. "And that was a relatively simple scene. What's going to happen when we do the love scenes?"

"The love scenes?" Kirk studied Ava intently. For the first time he noticed that her face had become flushed and her eyes had a wild look to them. "Why should that bother you especially?"

"Because..." Ava took a long steadying breath. She couldn't understand why she was having so much trouble telling Kirk the truth about her and Derek. "Kirk, you remember last night I told you that—"

"I'm not interrupting anything, am I?" Derek interrupted.

Ava's breath snagged when she turned to look over at him. He was standing with charming nonchalance in the doorway, one hand on the handle of the sword dangling from a leather strap on his left hip. She wondered how long he'd been standing there and how much of the conversation he'd overheard.

"As a matter of fact we were just talking about you, Derek," Kirk admitted openly.

"I thought I heard my name mentioned." Derek sent Ava an ironic smile as he sauntered over to them. "I have to pass your dressing room to get to mine and your door is open."

"Then you know what the problem is," Kirk said.

"Yes," Derek told Ava. "I know what the problem is."

"You really can't blame Ava for feeling the way she does," Kirk was quick to add in her defense. "She's the one who has to act opposite you."

"But this has nothing to do with my acting," Derek returned wryly. "Does it, Ava?"

"No," she admitted.

"Naturally no one's questioning your acting ability," Kirk began when Barry Jones, the A.D. came bursting into the room.

"I was hoping I'd find you here, Mr. Falconer," he said, gasping for breath. He'd obviously run down the entire flight of stairs to the dressing room.

Barry was a short, wiry bundle of nervous energy; he never walked when he could run, or sat when he could stand.

"Hal needs you right away," he said loudly. He always sounded as though he were talking through an invisible megaphone.

"Why?" Kirk demanded. "What happened now?"

"Well, you know Sam, the gaffer? He was trying to drive some hooks into the walls to hold up the spots?" A sigh of utter frustration escaped him. "So this Italian— he's the curator of the castle or something—he won't let him do it. He's having a conniption fit. Hal thought maybe you could talk to him."

"Okay, I'll take care of it," Kirk said, his tone calm and reassuring. "Looks like you're on your own, Derek."

"But Kirk, I need you, too," Ava protested. The last thing she wanted was to be left alone with her ex-lover.

"Sorry, Ava, but I can only solve one problem at a time. Without the proper lighting we won't be able to match the shots, and then we'll have to reshoot the scene you just did." Resolutely he started toward the exit. "I'll be back as soon as I can. Meanwhile, the two of you try to work it out, will you?" With a few long-legged strides he was out the door ahead of the A.D.

"I'll let you know as soon as we're ready to shoot," Barry shouted over his shoulder as he hurried to keep up with Kirk.

A long, strained pause hung between Derek and Ava. Then he flashed her the devastating smile that had made him the idol of women all over the world. "Well, shall we try to work it out, as your husband so generously suggested?"

"There's nothing to work out, Derek," Ava returned coldly. "I refuse to work with you and that's all there is to it.'' There was a time when she couldn't have refused him anything. That time had passed.

He was looking at her as if she'd given him a stage reading he hadn't expected and was trying to decide how his character should react.

"You've changed," he said thoughtfully. "You've grown up since I saw you last. I kind of miss that sweet, innocent quality you used to have. It was one of the things I loved the most about you." His eyes moved over the light blue gown that clung to the full curves of her breasts and hips before falling in a wide pool of silk at her feet. "But you're even more beautiful than I remembered."

Ava smiled scornfully at his compliment. "You, on the other hand, haven't changed at all."

"Yes, I have," Derek insisted with uncharacteristic regret. "I only wish I were still the man you once knew and loved."

Reaching into the chamois purse hanging from the jeweled belt slung loosely around his narrow hips, he took out a pack of cigarettes and a lighter. His hands were unsteady when he lit up. Ava wondered whether it was a reaction to what he was feeling or an inspired bit of acting.

"Don't let the old song and dance routine fool you," he said, exhaling a long stream of smoke. "I can still pull it off when I have to, but that's not the real me anymore."

"Don't even try using that routine with me, Derek," Ava warned.

"You really have changed." He took a long hard pull on his cigarette and exhaled. "You didn't used to be vindictive."

"Vindictive?"

"What would you call using your influence as the producer's wife to get me thrown off the picture?" He tossed the pack of cigarettes and lighter on the makeup table behind her. "You can't tell me you're not trying to pay me back for breaking off our affair."

"That's not true!" Ava protested. "I can't work with you because if..." She stopped herself just in time.

She couldn't tell him that she'd never gotten over him, or that she was afraid working with him would revive the feelings she'd kept buried inside her. Feelings she'd have to revive, as an actress, in order to play the love scenes. And then, where would acting end and real life begin?

"But if that's what you want to believe, that I'm being vindictive..." She forced a careless shrug and turned away from him. "I couldn't care less."

"Ava, I don't blame you for hating me after what I did to you," Derek said ruefully. "God knows, I've never been able to forgive myself. I acted like a first-class jerk."

She turned back to him, her eyes wide with surprise.

"I'd never been in love before," he explained. "Or since for that matter, and it scared the hell out of me."

Ava laughed incredulously, a bit brokenly. "You left me, the way you did, because you loved me?"

"Yes. And because we were both getting too serious," he admitted. "I knew if I stayed I'd end up marrying you. I wanted to marry you." He took a quick, nervous drag on his cigarette. "But I'd seen how marriage and the responsibility of supporting a family can wreck an actor's career before it even gets started. I was ambitious and driven then. I wasn't about to let anything stand in the way of my making it big. Not even my love for you."

"If you really loved me, Derek," Ava countered, "we could have worked it out."

"Like your mother and father did?" He dropped the cigarette butt on the stone floor and squashed it with his foot. "I didn't want to end up a failure like your father,

Ava, blaming you for the rest of my life for destroying my dreams.''

"But I'm not like my mother," Ava reminded him proudly. "I've never cared about material things. And unlike my parents, you and I shared the same dreams." Her voice trailed off as she thought of the past with an aching sense of loss. "At least I thought we did."

"And I thought I was doing the right thing at the time."

"You could have at least told me you were leaving me, Derek! How could you just leave a message with my answering service?"

"I had to! Don't you see?" His eyes met hers, and held them imploringly. "If I saw you again, Ava, I never would have been able to leave. I was on the verge of my big break and nothing and no one was going to hold me back." He shook his head in self-disgust. "That's the kind of selfish jerk I was. Until I met you, all I'd ever cared about was being famous."

A wry smile twisted the fine line of his lips. "The irony is, once I became a success none of it meant a damn to me without you." He moved closer and Ava wanted to step back, but she couldn't. He held her by the sheer seductive power of his presence, the deep rich tone of his voice, mesmerizing her as he had countless audiences. "I couldn't stop thinking about you and how happy we'd been together. You don't know how many times I was tempted to pick up the phone and call you."

"Why didn't you?" Ava asked in a small voice.

"Because I despised myself for what I did to you," he said miserably. "I could just imagine how much more you despised me. I think that's why I started drinking." He moved closer still. "Please don't hate me, Ava." Reaching out, he traced the line of her face with trembling fingers.

Ava jumped back and bumped into the table, knocking over several bottles of makeup. "I've never hated you, Derek," she admitted as she struggled to regain control of herself. "But nothing you've said changes anything. It only makes it worse. I'm sorry, but I can't work with you." Unable to bear the destroyed look on his face, she turned away from him, but his image was waiting for her in the mirror.

"Ava, I know I made a lot of mistakes, but I've paid for them," he insisted. "I wrecked my career, and I destroyed the only meaningful relationship I ever had with a woman. But I swear to you I've changed."

His ability to affect her hadn't changed. Trying to harden herself against him, Ava began straightening up the bottles she'd knocked over.

"Believe me," he persisted, "if I've learned anything these past four months in the sanitarium, it's how immature and self-destructive I've been."

Her hand froze in midair and she looked up at him in the mirror. "You were in a sanitarium?"

"Yes. Didn't Kirk tell you that when he offered me the part of Paolo, it was with the stipulation that I go to a special clinic to dry out and get professional help?"

"No," she breathed. "He didn't."

"He even advanced me the money I was so broke." He moved to the side of the makeup chair she was standing in front of. "Do you think I could ever let Kirk down after what he did for me? I haven't even been able to get my agent on the phone for the past year."

Ava sank slowly down onto the chair. "I didn't realize you were in such trouble."

"I haven't made a movie in almost two years, and if I screw this one up, I'll never make a movie again." He went down on one knee beside her, bringing his face on a level with hers. "If I get thrown off this picture now, on my first day, do you know what everyone will say? Derek Granger got drunk again, or he had a fight with his director. I'll be finished in this business for good."

As a drowning man might reach out to keep from going under, he grabbed on to her hands. "Ava, please don't do this to me." As his eyes pleaded with her, Ava remembered that in their brilliant blue depths she'd seen her first look of love.

"All right, Derek," Ava relented, "but—"

"I knew you couldn't have changed that much!" he exclaimed. "You always were the sweetest thing in the world. I'll never forget this." He gave her one of his dazzling smiles. "Any more than I could forget what we had together."

"You've got to forget it, Derek, or we can't work together!" Pulling her hands away, Ava jumped up from the chair. "I'm married now."

Shaking from a barrage of contradictory emotions, Ava stepped out from behind the makeup table and walked quickly over to the open door.

"By the way," Derek asked, pulling himself slowly to his feet, "did you tell Kirk about us?"

"No." Ava drew in a long breath of fresh air, hoping it would calm her. "I was just about to tell him when you came in."

He nodded to himself while retrieving his cigarettes and lighter from the makeup table. "That's what I'd thought."

Ava slanted him a determined look. "I still intend to."

"I don't think that's such a good idea, Ava," Derek said, coming over to her.

"Why not?"

A slow seductive smile curved his mouth. "You really don't know?"

"No, I don't," she returned defensively. "I've always told Kirk the truth. I owe it to him." In an attempt to get away from Derek and the disturbing feelings he'd stirred up inside her, she stepped outside.

Derek followed. "Well, maybe you know what you're doing, but..." He paused when he caught sight of Kirk descending the marble stairway across the courtyard. "Strictly from a male point of view, if I had to watch my wife playing passionate love scenes with a man I knew she was in love with once, it would drive me crazy."

"Kirk's not like you," she assured him. "He's not an emotional person."

"Really?" Derek took a moment to light a cigarette. "My instinct about people tells me Kirk's a very possessive man." He took a thoughtful drag on his cigarette and sent a long stream of smoke spiraling up to the arched ceiling of the arcade. "I get the feeling that if his jealousy were ever aroused he could play Othello without make-up."

Ava laughed. She couldn't imagine Kirk letting himself care enough for a woman to be consumed by uncontrollable jealousy. But as she watched him turn the corner under the arcade she realized that she hadn't thought of him as being passionate, either—until last night.

"Kirk's not the jealous type," she insisted.

"I hope you're right," Derek said, watching Kirk walking toward them with quick, resolute steps. "I've certainly never met a man who exudes the confidence he does." His tone was openly envious. "Let's hope he feels that secure about your love."

Ava looked away.

"How's it going?" Derek called over to Kirk.

"We're all set," he called back. In a few, sure strides he was by their side.

"We're all set, too," Derek declared proudly.

Remembering how upset Ava had been at the prospect of working with Derek, Kirk looked at her in surprise. "You've changed your mind?"

Ava nodded stiffly.

"I'm delighted you've settled this," Kirk said sincerely, "because I know you're going to work beautifully together."

"We always have," Derek exhaled on a long stream of smoke.

Kirk looked questioningly from Derek to Ava. "You've worked together before?"

"We belonged to the same acting class," Derek explained, flicking the cigarette butt through the sweeping arch into the courtyard. "We did quite a few scenes together. Didn't we, Ava?"

Ava was unable to answer. She felt as though she were stuck in the wrong play with the wrong lines. All she could do was watch the growing awareness in Kirk's eyes, the rugged lines of his face tighten.

Derek laughed with great satisfaction. "They're still talking about our balcony scene from *Romeo and Juliet*."

"Yes, I'm sure they are," Kirk said. His tone was all the more chilling for being utterly devoid of emotion.

Seven

The rest of the afternoon was spent working on the film. Ironically, the conflicting emotions Ava had experienced during her encounter with Derek were the very ones she needed to enact Francesca's feelings about seeing Paolo again. But another feeling kept creeping into her work, one she hadn't explored during her preparation for the part: a sense of guilt in relation to her husband.

The few times Kirk spoke to her, it was on a purely professional level, and his manner was polite but distant. She was sure he'd wait until they got back to the villa that evening before demanding an explanation about Derek. She felt sorry that he'd found out the way he had. She'd wanted to tell him herself.

But when she'd finished removing her makeup and had changed back into her street clothes he'd sent the A.D. to inform her that Marco would drive her back to the villa by herself. She was not to hold dinner for him as he'd be

spending the better part of the evening going over storyboards on the next day's scenes with Hal and "Dutch"
Hermann, the director of photography.

On their way back to the villa, Ava had Marco stop the
car across from the cypress grove where Kirk had flung the
emerald pendant. It took almost half an hour in the dwin-
dling twilight, but she finally located the velvet box among
the wild grasses.

After returning to the villa, Ava took a leisurely bath to
dissolve the tension in her back. The sunken bathtub was
more like a black marble pool with solid brass fixtures.
Feeling a little more relaxed, she went down to dinner.

Kirk still hadn't returned by the time Ava had had a
second cup of espresso laced with anisette. Feeling a bit
lost, she decided to make her first complete tour of her
temporary home. Every room had been painstakingly re-
stored. Each one was a work of art in itself, while housing
a dizzying array of Renaissance paintings and sculptures
and beautifully crafted furnishings. Every wide, ceiling-
high window framed seascapes shimmering in the moonlight.

While she waited in the living room for Kirk's return,
Ava tried to work on her lines for the next day's scenes but
was unable to concentrate. She found herself memorizing
words of explanation, instead. It was eleven o'clock before she finally gave up on being able to sort everything out
involving Kirk and Derek and went upstairs. But lying in
the very bed she'd made love in with Kirk the night before
only added a sensual element to her thoughts, making it
impossible for her to fall asleep.

When she thought of what it had been like making love
with Derek, she could only recall her love for him, that
wonderfully delirious joy of discovering love for the first
time. Utterly captivated, she was forever touching him in

her inexperienced but eager way, pouring adoring kisses over his beautiful face and body.

But when she thought of Kirk, she remembered how he'd made love to her. She could still feel his hands on her skin, his mouth devouring every part of her with kisses, the full burning extent of his possession. Her response to him had been so complete it couldn't be recaptured by thought, but lingered somewhere in the deepest recesses of her being.

With an exasperated sigh, Ava sat up against the pillows and switched the lights back on. She simply couldn't understand how sex without love could be so overwhelming.

Impulsively, she threw off the covers and jumped out of bed. Maybe working on her lines would stop her from thinking so much. Having retrieved her script, she was searching through her oversize handbag for a pen, when her hand brushed up against the velvet jewelry box she'd tossed inside earlier. Taking it out, she opened it, and the dazzling emerald caught the light, splintering it into glittering green shards.

Yet all Ava could see was the hurt reflected in Kirk's eyes as he'd savagely thrown the pendant out the car window. *"Services rendered? Is that all you think last night meant to me?"* For several minutes she stared at his extravagant gift as though she were seeing it for the first time. *"You don't want anything I have to give, least of all my love."*

Feeling more confused than ever, Ava closed the velvet box. Brushing a smudge of earth off one corner, she was setting it on top of the dresser just as she heard footsteps coming down the hall outside. From the strong, sure sound of them, they could have belonged only to Kirk. When they came to a sudden halt in front of her door, she realized she had forgotten to breathe.

Kirk hesitated at the closed door, although the ribbon of light at its edge assured him that Ava was still awake. He told himself it would be better to talk about Derek in the morning, when he was less tired and better able to control his emotions. He was afraid of what he might do. He spun on his heel and quickly crossed the hallway to his bedroom.

As he was reaching for the brass handle on his door, Ava's door opened and she stepped out into the hall. "Kirk?"

"Yes?" He turned toward her and his heart slammed up against his rib cage. The bedroom light spilling through the doorway behind her rendered the filmy layers of her white nightgown transparent, silhouetting every lovely curve of her body. For an instant he thought it a typically female ploy, but then he realized that she was unaware of how seductive she looked. Her exquisite face registered only confusion, and she seemed unable to explain why she'd called him.

All the carefully rehearsed words of explanation had flown out of Ava's head at the sight of Kirk. She suddenly understood why she'd had so much trouble telling him about Derek earlier: she didn't want to hurt him anymore than she already had by refusing his gift. She hadn't known, until the incident in the car, that he could be hurt by her.

"I didn't realize you were going to work so late," was all she could finally say to break the tense silence between them.

"We had a lot of work to do."

"Did you have dinner?"

A sarcastic smile twisted his mouth. "Such wifely concern is truly touching. We had room service send up something."

His sarcasm made her withdraw even more into herself. Another long pause hung between them, heavy with the subject they both found too difficult to put into words.

"I didn't think you'd still be awake," Kirk said. "It's after midnight. You should be in bed. You've got a 7:00 a.m. wake-up call."

"I waited up for you." Ava said, swallowing hard. "I wanted to explain about this afternoon, about Derek."

"It's a bit late for that, isn't it?" he returned flatly. "You didn't seem to be in any hurry to tell me about him before. I'm sure this can wait till tomorrow."

"No, it can't." She took a step toward him, layers of her gown swirling around her legs. "Kirk, please. I won't be able to sleep unless we talk about it."

Knowing how Ava preferred to evade problems, Kirk was surprised by her determination. "All right."

Though he tried, he couldn't take his eyes off the softly feminine sway of her hips as he followed her into her bedroom. He remembered the feel of her under his hands—Derek had also known her unforgettable softness and warmth. He couldn't ignore the pain knowing that brought him.

"So Derek Granger has the honor of being your one and only love," he got out caustically before she could say a word.

"Yes," Ava admitted with difficulty. "I'm really sorry you found out about it the way you did, Kirk." Wanting to show him that she meant what she'd said, she put her hand softly on his arm. He stiffened at her touch. "I started to tell you about Derek and me, but—"

"When was that?" he cut her off, pulling his arm away. It was bad enough she'd made a fool out of him; she didn't have to lie to him on top of it. "I must have missed something." Turning, he walked away from her. He needed to put some distance between them in order to keep his emotions under control.

"Earlier this afternoon in the dressing room," she reminded him. "I was just on the verge of telling you, when Derek came in."

"Derek always did have a great sense of timing," he allowed dryly, "and he certainly knows how to make an entrance, but..." He came to a sudden halt in front of the dresser. "How did that get there?" Reaching out, he picked up the black velvet box.

"I remembered more or less where it landed," Ava explained, going over to him. "So on my way home tonight I searched for it and found it."

He looked at her directly for the first time since his arrival, and when he spoke it was without sarcasm. "Does this mean you're willing to accept my gift?"

"No, I just..." She saw his hand tighten dangerously around the box. "But that's no reason to throw it out the window again! Give it to me!" He let her pull the box out of his hand, and she tucked it safely into the top drawer of the dresser before continuing. "Kirk, I've never lied to you." She looked up into his eyes, not expecting the coldness she saw there. "How could I have known this would happen?"

He laughed harshly. "It's like a scene in a bad movie."

"I had every intention of telling you about Derek," she insisted. "If I'd only known you were planning to cast him as Paolo, I'd have told you what the situation was then."

He held her gaze for a long moment. "Tell me what the situation is now, Ava," he said evenly. "Are you still in love with him?"

She dropped her eyes. "I don't know," she admitted, her voice barely audible. "I only know I don't want to love him."

"Just because you want to stop loving someone doesn't mean you can," Kirk muttered with a trace of bitterness. In spite of the pain she was causing him, he'd never wanted her more. He ached to bury himself deep inside her, to burn her down to her bones and wipe Derek Granger out of her mind and heart forever.

If only it were that simple.

"So where do we go from here?" he managed coolly. "Are you planning on picking up where you left off with Derek?"

"No, of course not," Ava cried, hurt that he would think that of her. "I don't even want to work with him. Why do you think I begged you to replace him with John Colby?"

"Because Derek still has an effect on you," Kirk said, his voice tight. With intense eyes he searched hers. "He does, doesn't he?"

"Oh, I don't know," Ava said miserably, walking away. For five years Derek had haunted her fantasies, and she'd been sure of her love for him—until last night. "I'm just so confused."

"If you really don't want to work with him," Kirk persisted, following her, "then why did you let him change your mind about it?"

"What else could I do?" She halted beside the chaise lounge. "He told me how he just got out of a sanitarium, and how he hasn't made a movie in two years. If he's replaced now everyone will assume it's because he was drunk. He'll never work again." With a defeated sigh, she sank down on the chaise. "I couldn't do that to him."

"After what he did to you," Kirk reminded her sharply, "I would think you'd be delighted for the chance to get even with him."

"It's not just him," Ava protested. "I couldn't do that to anyone!"

"No, I know you couldn't," Kirk acknowledged softly. He knew she was incapable of kicking a man when he was down—even if he deserved it. Obviously Derek knew that about her, as well, and hadn't hesitated to use that for his own purposes.

"I realize it's what makes you such a wonderful actress, Ava," he added wryly, sitting down next to her, "but sometimes I think you're too sensitive for your own good." He failed to add that her sensitivity was one of the reasons he loved her.

"*You're* the one who took a chance on him when no one else would, Kirk. Could you replace him?"

"Yes, I could," he stated unequivocally. "And I will if I have to."

"Then why don't you?"

A wry smile tugged at the corners of his mouth. "You'd like that, wouldn't you, Ava, having me take care of the problem for you?" He shook his head slowly. "But I'm not going to. I hired Derek to do a job. If he doesn't do that job then I'll fire him. I'm not about to fire a man because my wife may still be in love with him."

Ava's lips parted at his startling statement, but she was unable to reply.

"Besides—" he leaned toward her "—I know I can't win against the fantasy image you obviously have of Derek. But I think I stand a chance against the real man."

It was just like him to think in terms of winning, Ava thought resentfully, she might have been a prize he was competing for. Love had no part in that prize. She turned away from him.

"I'm not going to give you up without a fight," he vowed fiercely. "You're my wife now, and I want you."

Reaching out, he grabbed her by the shoulders and turned her back to him. His hands held her possessively, making her feel like an object that he owned and refused to relinquish. His fingers burned on her bare flesh. "But *you're* the one who's going to have to decide whether you want our marriage to work, Ava. That's entirely your decision."

"My decision?" She pulled away from him. The heat from his touch lingered disturbingly on her skin, increasing her sense of powerlessness and resentment. "Since when have I had anything to say about it?"

"Since when?" He smiled crookedly. "Since the beginning. You've always been free to make your own choices."

Ava jumped to her feet angrily. "If I'd been free to make my own choice I would never have married you!"

Kirk flinched as her words struck him hard. He forced a sardonic smile. "All you had to do was say no."

"I did say no, but you wouldn't take no for an answer!"

"I never take no for an answer when I want something badly enough," he returned harshly. "I wanted you to be my wife. That was *my* choice. But *you* agreed!" With one angry motion he was on his feet before her. "For whatever reason, you made the choice to marry me. And one of these days you're going to have to admit that to yourself and take the responsibility for it!"

"You never gave me a choice," Ava insisted bitterly. Until that moment, she hadn't realized how much she'd held that against him.

"I didn't exactly tie you up and drag you kicking and screaming to the altar, did I?"

"You did the next best thing," she shot back. "You got together with my father, knowing how—"

"What the hell are you talking about?" he cut her off savagely. "I never got together with your father. I don't even like your father."

Ava stared at Kirk uncomprehendingly. "You didn't promise Mike you'd make me a star if he'd convince me to marry you?"

"The only time I spoke to your father about us was after you'd agreed to marry me," he informed her proudly. "I never needed your father's approval. And I think it's disgraceful the way he exploits you."

"Exploits me? He's only trying to help me," Ava returned defensively. She felt as though he'd touched a sore spot she hadn't known was there. "My father loves me!"

"He may love you," Kirk allowed dryly, "but that doesn't stop him from exploiting you. And you let him."

"You don't know anything about my father," Ava cried, her voice shaking. "You don't know all the sacrifices he's made for me. He ruined his own acting career. For years he worked at jobs he hated because he had to support me. Because of me my mother left him!"

"Because of you?"

"Yes. There was never enough money, but every extra cent he made he spent on me," she explained painfully. "Acting lessons and voice and dancing lessons and...and it always made my mother furious. They fought day and night over me." Tears burned behind her eyes and she struggled to hold them back. "He was devastated when she left him. He still hasn't gotten over it."

Kirk saw the anguish on Ava's face, and he forgot he was angry at her. "Why do you blame yourself?" he asked softly. "It seems to me your mother was furious at your father because he was trying to exploit his own child—*her* child."

That was a possibility Ava had never considered, and she pushed the traitorous thought resolutely out of her mind. "You still don't understand about Mike. All his dreams of being a success have gone up in smoke. *My* success is the only dream he has left."

"So *that's* why you agreed to marry me," Kirk murmured as if to himself.

He'd always assumed that, like the actresses he'd been involved with before her, Ava was merely interested in using his power and influence to selfishly further her career. He should have known better. He had only to recall last night to realize that she was incapable of using sex to get ahead.

"Why me?" he asked her.

Ava looked up at Kirk with surprise. "What?"

"You're a very beautiful woman, Ava." His eyes slid over the lush curves her nightgown barely concealed. "I'm sure you must have had offers from other producers. They may not have included marriage, but I'm willing to bet that wouldn't have bothered your father." The pained look that flickered across her face told Kirk his hunch had been correct. "Did you accept any of those offers?"

"No, of course not," Ava replied, offended. "I even lost out on several parts because I refused to go to bed with the right people."

"Then let me repeat the question. Why me?"

"Because I felt safe with you," she said without hesitation.

He smiled crookedly. No one had ever accused him of that before. "Safe?"

"Yes," Ava admitted, her voice calm and sure as she went on to list the reasons she'd always given herself for marrying Kirk. "You always treated me with respect. You made me feel you really believed in my talent. And I'd always admired you tremendously...because of your work. And, of course, I knew how much my marrying you meant to Mike.''

''It all sounds perfectly logical,'' Kirk allowed wryly. He took a step toward her. ''But how do you explain your response to me last night?''

Ava had no explanation. That's what bothered her the most about it. ''Well, you must admit you're a very compelling man, Kirk,'' she said, determined to find a logical reason for the sensual abandon he'd brought her to. ''You completely overwhelmed me.''

''So *you* had absolutely nothing to do with it,'' he drawled sardonically. ''I didn't give you a choice last night, either, is that what you're saying?''

''Well...yes.''

''But I told you to feel free to stop me anytime you wanted,'' he reminded her. ''You didn't stop me.''

''How could I?'' she protested. ''I couldn't even think straight.''

''No, I know you couldn't. You were too busy feeling.'' A smile of pure male satisfaction curved his lips and glowed in his dark eyes as they locked with hers. ''You didn't just go through the motions with me, Ava. You wanted me as much as I wanted you.''

Maybe more, Ava realized to her own amazement, since all he'd wanted was sex. She wasn't about to give him the satisfaction of knowing that. ''No, I didn't,'' she lied defensively, brushing past him.

''The hell you didn't!'' he grated, stepping quickly in front of her to stop her from walking away, forcing her to deal with him. ''What do I have to do to get you to admit it?'' He didn't wait for an answer. Instead he brusquely grabbed her waist and pulled her up against him as his mouth came down on hers.

Before she could recover, he slid his other hand into her hair, making it impossible for her to pull her head away. He held her firmly but gently, as though he wanted her to know he had no intention of forcing a response from her, and his mouth moved on hers softly.

She didn't fight him. She let him go on kissing her to prove to him—and even more to herself—that she could resist him. With long, slow strokes of his tongue he parted her lips and slipped inside. She managed to stifle a moan as he slid his tongue wetly over hers, but when it plunged deep inside, her whole body contracted against his.

His kiss went out of control. The hunger he no longer bothered to deny shuddered through her, as well. She had to grab on to him. She could feel herself slipping away from herself and there was nothing she could do about it. The passionate intensity coiling every muscle in his body shattered what little resistance she had left. He eased his hand out of her hair and moved searchingly down her gown.

A groan tore out of him, mingling with hers, when his hand closed possessively around her breast, burning through the filmy fabric. Unerringly his fingers found the swollen tip. He dragged his mouth away from hers. "Your body knows how much you want me even if you don't," he muttered triumphantly.

With one quick stroke he brushed the delicate strap off her shoulder, sending the triangle of lace shivering down her breast. Bending his head, he took the peak into his mouth, surrounding it. Slowly at first, he swirled warm wet caresses over her, drawing out the pleasure it gave her almost unendurably. Then, driven by his own need he tightened his lips around her and he tugged on her fiercely, ravenously, until she shuddered with excitement.

He smiled with deep satisfaction when he finally lifted his mouth and saw that she was trembling all over, too dazed with passion even to speak.

"I could do just about anything to you right now, couldn't I?" he asked thickly. "I know what I'd like to do." The hunger burning in his eyes left no doubt as to his intentions and his hand glided down her body to caress her intimately. "But I wouldn't want you to accuse me of not giving you a choice again." His hand slid off her. "When you're ready to admit that you want me as much as I want you, *you'll* have to come to me."

He sounded infuriatingly sure of himself, but his fingers were shaking when they lifted her shoulder strap back in place, pulling the lacy covering over her bare breast. "My bedroom is just across the hall," he reminded her. "I'll be waiting for you."

Kirk never knew where he found the strength to leave Ava standing there, her eyes wide, her face flushed with desire. He only knew that he wanted her to give herself to him of her own free will—or not at all.

It took Ava several moments to recover. She felt betrayed by her own body. She could still feel the blood pounding at every pulse point, the liquid heat flowing through her, leaving an emptiness deep inside that ached to be filled. She was furious with him for gloating over the power he had, but she was no longer able to deny how much she wanted him.

It would have been so easy to go to him then, so easy to make herself believe that the longing she'd seen in his eyes and had felt in his every touch had anything to do with love. She was surprised to find how much she wanted to believe that. But she had to remind herself that although Kirk wanted her to give herself to him completely, he had no intention of giving himself in return.

Slowly she turned and walked over to her bed.

His body aching for her, Kirk waited for the knock on his bedroom door that never came.

Eight

The strain was beginning to get to him, Kirk realized when he'd set the coffee cup down so hard it almost cracked the saucer. Every night for the past two weeks he'd waited for Ava to come to him. Every night he'd ended up alone in bed, tossing and turning until he fell into a restless sleep. Even in his dreams she evaded him.

Mornings he awoke aroused, unable to dispel the longing for her that suffused his dreams, the love she wanted no part of. Seeing her all the time without being able to touch her increased his frustration. It had been difficult enough keeping his hands off her before they were married, but now that he knew what it was like making love with her, it was rapidly driving him up the wall.

"Another cup of coffee, Signor Kirk?" Marina asked.

Kirk had been so deep in thought he hadn't heard her come back into the dining room. "No, thanks, Marina."

"What is this?" the housekeeper demanded when she halted in front of the table. With a sweeping wave of her hand, she indicated his half-eaten breakfast. "The *frittata* was not to your liking this morning, Signor Kirk?"

"It was fine," he assured her, pushing his plate away. "I'm just not hungry."

"In Italy we have a proverb." Resolutely she slid the *frittata* of eggs, mushrooms and zucchini back in front of him. "Appetite comes with eating."

"So true," Kirk allowed with a wry smile. But the appetite he'd been thinking about had nothing to do with food. He pushed his plate away again.

"No one is hungry in this house," she grumbled. "The *signora* ate like a sick bird last night, and this morning she did not even touch her *caffelatte*."

"It's probably nerves," Kirk said tightly. "We're shooting the big scene today."

"But then she needs twice as much strength. She should—" Her words broke off when she caught sight of Ava in the doorway. "Ah, *eccola*." Her large dark eyes lit up and she hurried off to greet her.

Adjusting the strap on her oversize handbag, Ava sent Kirk a strained smile. "Good morning, Kirk."

"Good morning," he returned without looking at her. It was easier when he didn't look at her. Pushing away from the table he got to his feet.

"Signora Ava, are you sure I cannot get you a little something to eat?"

"No, thanks, Marina."

Kirk picked up on the tension in Ava's voice instantly. As he walked over to her, he noted that her skin was unnaturally pale and there were dark shadows under her eyes. If she was having trouble sleeping, he reminded himself bitterly, it wasn't because of him.

"I'm afraid I can't eat a thing."

"Butterflies?" Kirk drawled sarcastically. "That's right, we're shooting the big love scene today." Just the thought of Ava being touched by Derek sent pain slicing through him and made him want to lash out at her. "But I thought you'd enjoy that."

Her sharp intake of breath was all the answer Ava was capable of.

"Let's go," Kirk ordered, ignoring the strange look Marina was giving him. "I'm sure you don't want to be late today of all days."

"Signor Kirk, will you and the *signora* be having dinner at home tonight?" Marina asked carefully as Kirk was about to lead Ava out the door.

"Were you planning on eating home tonight, Ava?" Kirk's tone couldn't have been more indifferent.

"Of course," Ava snapped, unable to hold back her irritation any longer. She was surprised he had to ask. She always ate dinner at home. *He* was the one who hadn't been home for dinner one night last week because he worked late. Last night he hadn't come home until after midnight. She was beginning to wonder whether he was really working. It bothered her that she cared.

"I won't be here," Kirk informed Marina. "I'm flying to Rome this morning. I'll be back in a couple of days."

"Rome?" Ava gasped.

"Yes. We'd better hurry. *Ciao*, Marina." Taking Ava's arm, he propelled her out the door ahead of him. "Marco has barely enough time to drop you off at the set before taking me on to the airport in Rimini."

"Why didn't you tell me you were going to Rome?" Ava protested.

He slanted her a sardonic look. "Why? Will you miss me?"

"Kirk, you can't go to Rome." Ava came to an abrupt halt in the middle of the marble foyer. "Not today. I need you."

"You don't need me, Ava."

"But I do," she admitted a bit frantically. "You know how much it means to me to have you on the set. Your opinion is more important to me than anyone else's...even Hal's."

He let out a short, sardonic laugh as he continued over to the door. "Thanks a lot. It's great to be needed."

"I don't understand," she persisted, following him. "Why do you have to go to Rome today?"

"Because I have a meeting with the European distributor of the film."

"But you could postpone your meeting till tomorrow or the next day." She grabbed his arm just as he was reaching for the door handle. "Kirk, please don't go."

It was the first time she'd touched him in two weeks. He could feel the pressure of her fingers through his suit jacket. It reminded him of the way she'd dug her nails into him when he'd made love to her. He drew in a harsh breath. "Why not?"

Ava hesitated. She wanted to tell Kirk how much she dreaded doing the love scene with Derek, but that would be admitting Derek still had an effect on her. Somehow, just knowing that Kirk would be there made her feel more safe.

The fear darkening Ava's eyes wasn't lost on Kirk. He knew she was afraid that doing the love scene with Derek might revive the love she once had for him. It was the same fear that had kept him awake most of last night.

"Why not, Ava?" he repeated, his voice hard.

"Because it's the most important scene in the movie, Kirk, and the most difficult one for me." Her fingers tightened around his arm imploringly. "I need you to be there."

He was surprised that she'd want him to be there. Though he couldn't figure out her motive, her sincerity was undeniable. But he could have sooner walked through fire than put himself through the ordeal of watching Ava and Derek recreate the passion they'd once shared.

"I'm sure you can handle it," he managed matter-of-factly. "Hal's a very good director. He's especially good at love scenes." He shook her hand off. "Besides," he added caustically before he could stop himself, "I'm sure Derek will be a great help."

Ava stepped back. For a long moment she stared at him. "Why are you doing this?" she asked, her voice barely audible. "Don't you realize what you're doing?"

No one realized the gamble he was taking better than Kirk. Or how much he had to lose if he was wrong.

"If we don't leave now I'll miss my plane," he said harshly, "and you'll be late for the shoot." Pulling the door open, he stepped outside. He didn't wait for her. With long, impatient strides he started toward the limousine idling in the driveway.

"Mike, I'm fine," Ava insisted, forcing a bright smile for her father's benefit. "I'm just nervous. You know how I get before a big scene."

His brows knitted under the dark bangs of his page boy wig while he studied her critically. The black-and-gold quilted velvet tunic he wore made his torso appear broader than it was and gave his frail figure more authority than it naturally possessed.

"Why isn't Kirk here?" he demanded, resuming his restless pacing. "That's what I'd like to know."

It was an effort for Ava to keep her tone casual. "I told you, he had an important meeting with the European distributor in Rome."

"I don't get it. He's on set for the most insignificant little scene and today when you're going to shoot the most important..." He halted in front of the wrought iron daybed where Ava was lying, propped up against a low, thick cushion so as not to spoil her intricately styled medieval hairdo. "You didn't have a fight with him, did you?"

"Mike, please," Ava pleaded, her nerves raw. If she thought about Kirk now she wouldn't be able to function at all. "My scene is up next. I'm trying to work on my preparation and—"

"That's it, isn't it?" he cut her off accusingly. "What did you do to upset him?"

Ava stared at her father for several moments, suddenly feeling he was a stranger. "Why don't you ask whether he did something to upset me?"

"Oh, my God," he exclaimed, horrified. "I was right. What happened?" He held a frail hand up in front of him as if to ward off a blow. "Don't tell me. I don't want to know." With great dramatic effect, he shook his fist at the merciless heavens. "And just when everything was going so great for us!"

"Don't look now, Mike," a perfectly modulated voice interjected from the doorway, "but I spy more trouble coming your way."

"What do *you* want, Derek?" Mike never bothered to hide the resentment he still felt toward his daughter's ex-lover.

Derek nodded in the direction of the arcade. "I just thought you'd like to know that the A.D. is hot on your trail."

"Don't worry about me." A disapproving frown tightened the deeply etched lines between his brows as he took in Derek's half-dressed state. "Shouldn't you finish getting into costume?"

"This is as far as I go until they're ready to shoot," Derek explained, indicating his dancer's tights and the white silk shirt with long, billowing sleeves that was gathered around his waist by an elasticized band. He was in full makeup, also, and Kleenex tissues were tucked around the deeply slashed, open neckline of his shirt to protect it. A gold medallion gleamed amid the black curls on his chest. Although he was wearing a jockstrap, his peacock-blue tights left little to the imagination.

He seemed to find Mike's disapproving frown amusing. "Wardrobe will murder me if I crease my tunic and she has to iron it all over again."

That was the reason Ava was wearing her robe instead of her costume. She suddenly felt undressed and checked to make sure her robe was properly closed.

Derek smiled.

"This is Ava's dressing room," Mike informed him belligerently. "Why don't you wait for your call in your own?"

"I could say the same to you, Mike," the A.D. told him irritably as he brushed past Derek. "How many times do I have to tell you I can't keep running up and down those stairs after you?"

"Kirk told me to stay with Ava while he's away," Mike lied grandly.

"Well, do it during someone else's scene. You're holding up production." Spinning around, the A.D. went rushing back out the door. "Let's go."

Mike gave Ava a quick fatherly pat on the shoulder. "Now don't you worry about a thing, princess. Everything's going to be great. If you have any trouble with anything or anybody, just let me know." He shot Derek a warning look as he passed him. "And I'll tell Kirk." Twirling the end of his cape dramatically over one arm, he hurried to keep up with the A.D.

"I'm afraid your father still doesn't approve of me," Derek said as he watched the two men turn the corner under the arcade. "I really can't blame him," he added, looking over at Ava with a disarming grin. "I am a rather disreputable character."

"Yes, you are," Ava agreed soberly.

"Don't tell me *you* no longer approve of me. You're the only one who ever has." He let out a mock tragic sigh. "And I tried so hard to be good these past few weeks." His eyes slid over her semireclining figure. "It hasn't been easy."

"Derek, if you don't mind, I'd like to be alone," Ava said coolly. With tense fingers she opened the script that was resting on her lap. "I still have work to do on the scene."

"Maybe I can help," he offered, stepping inside her dressing room. "Why are you having so much trouble with our scene?"

"I'm not having any trouble with it," she assured him, flipping through the script to her entrance. "It just needs more work."

"You were pretty uptight during the run-through earlier." Pulling the tissues from around his collar, he wadded them in his hand, tossing them onto the makeup table as he walked over to her. "I felt like I was holding a statue in my arms. A very beautiful, cold, marble statue." He stopped in front of the daybed. "That's not like you."

"It was just a run-through," she reminded him. "I didn't want to lose it in rehearsal. I was saving my feelings for when we actually do the scene."

He laughed softly. "I can hardly wait."

His seductive manner brought up emotions Ava was willing to explore only during their love scene. She wasn't sure she could handle them in reality. "Will you please leave me alone so I can work on my preparation?"

He cocked his head and gave her a look from beneath his long thick lashes. "Why do you keep trying to avoid me?"

"I haven't been trying to avoid you," she lied.

"You haven't said more than two words to me off camera in as many weeks," he insisted. "This is the first chance I've had to talk to you alone. If Kirk isn't always hovering around you, your father is."

With the eye-baffling ease of a magician, his hand produced a pack of cigarettes and a lighter from beneath the deep folds of his shirt. "You disappear the instant we break for the day, and you've never once joined the cast and crew on any of our get-togethers at the hotel in the evenings."

"I've been too busy," she murmured evasively.

"Doing what?" A wry smile played on his lips as he slowly tapped a cigarette out of the pack. "What do you do nights all by yourself?"

Ava was thrown for a moment. How did he know she'd been spending her nights alone? "What makes you say that?"

"Well, I know Kirk's been working late with Hal and 'Dutch' at the hotel every night."

"He does have a movie to produce," she pointed out defensively.

"That's true." He paused to light a cigarette and send a long, thoughtful stream of smoke up to the arched ceiling. "It hasn't been much of a honeymoon for you, has it?"

"Kirk and I decided to postpone our honeymoon until we wrap the film," Ava returned with what she hoped was a casual shrug.

Derek took a long pull on his cigarette and let out a perfect ring of smoke. He watched the ring, widening as it rose, until it dissolved in space. "I still don't know how he does it. *I* couldn't." He lowered himself smoothly onto the edge of the bed next to her. "If I had you waiting for me at home, you couldn't get me to work nights if you held a gun to my head."

Ava tensed in reaction to the closeness of Derek's body. His tights were like a second skin, emphasizing the sleekly toned muscles of his long legs and tight buttocks. She was about to tell him to get up from the bed, but she didn't want him to know that he still had the power to affect her.

"I told you once before, Derek," she said, shifting her position to put more distance between them, "Kirk isn't like you. He's a very responsible man. He knows how much everyone involved in this production depends on him."

The look he slid her seemed to question whom she was trying to convince, him or herself.

"He's totally dedicated to making every film he produces a work of art," she rattled on. "You know how he insists on supervising everything down to the smallest detail."

Derek tossed his cigarette pack and lighter onto the bed ever so casually. "That's why I can't understand why he isn't here today."

"He had an important business meeting in Rome with the European distributor of the film," she explained for the tenth time that morning.

"So I heard." He didn't sound convinced. With one tap of his index finger, he flicked ash onto the stone floor. "But why did he make the appointment for today?"

"Obviously the distributor couldn't make it any other time."

Derek shook his dark curly head. "That's not like Kirk, either. He doesn't make time for other people—they make time for him."

Ava was unable to argue that point, and she gave up trying to find an excuse for Kirk's conspicuous absence. She still couldn't understand why he'd deliberately chosen to leave her alone with her ex-lover, even though she'd begged him not to.

Derek drew in a quick puff and exhaled sharply as though a thought had suddenly occurred to him. "You said you were going to tell Kirk about us. Did you?"

"Yes, of course."

"I figured that's why his manner toward me had cooled," he murmured under his breath. "But the pieces still don't fit the puzzle. If Kirk knows we were lovers, that's one more reason he should be here today." He leaned toward her, sending the gold medallion sliding over the dark curls on his chest.

Ava suddenly recalled how silky they felt between her fingers.

"If you were *my* wife," he assured her, "and you were going to do a passionate love scene with a man you once loved, the last thing I'd do is leave the two of you alone together." Dropping the cigarette butt on the floor, he squashed it under his suede boot. "Especially when he must know you're not in love with him."

Ava pulled back against the cushion. "What makes you so sure of that?"

"Because I've seen you in love, Ava," he reminded her softly, sensuously. "I remember the look of love on your face whenever you were with me. I've never been able to forget it." He smiled. "And I've never once seen you look at Kirk that way."

"You're remembering a girl who doesn't exist anymore, Derek. I couldn't love anyone like that again." She laughed, a short bitter laugh. "Not even you."

He stared at her intently, his brilliant blue eyes darkening with regret. "Did *I* do that to you?" Reaching out, he traced the line of her cheek tenderly. "I'm sorry."

"Don't be," Ava said, pushing his hand away. "You taught me a lesson I needed to learn. One I don't intend to forget. Women want love—men *only* want sex. Their work is all men really care about."

"I was like that once," Derek admitted, "but not anymore. And I really loved you, Ava. I still do."

"I've also learned that there are more important things in a relationship than what you men call *love*."

He grinned appealingly. "Name one."

"Respect. Trust. Having someone who believes in you," she told him. "I have all those things with Kirk. It's true, I'm not in love with him, but I've never admired a man as much as I admire him."

"Hey, you don't have to sell me on Kirk," Derek said. "I could never forget what he's done for me. I think the world of him."

"I'm sure you mean that," she allowed wryly. "But you'd betray him with me in a second, wouldn't you?"

"I can't help it if I'm in love with you," Derek protested. "If I thought he really loved you, I wouldn't be saying any of this."

"That's enough, Derek!"

Tossing her script aside, Ava moved to get to her feet, but Derek was too quick for her. With a fencer's lunge, he parried her body with his. Intricately curved wrought iron bars enclosed the other three sides of the daybed. Unless she was willing to physically struggle with him—and she wasn't—there was no other avenue of escape.

"You know I'm right, Ava," he insisted, grabbing onto a wrought iron curlicue next to her shoulder, creating another barrier with his arm. "If Kirk really loves you then why does he work late every night when he should be with you? And why isn't he here with you now, instead of at some business meeting?"

Ava sank back against the cushion. She didn't bother to answer Derek, since the answer was as obvious as it was painful. Kirk *didn't* love her, except in the only way men loved women. His work was all he cared about. She couldn't understand why that should bother her so much, since that was one of the reasons she'd agreed to marry him. She'd never felt so confused in her life.

"Look, I'm not trying to put Kirk down," Derek went on. "It's just that I can't see you with someone like him. I realize he's got money and power and he can do a lot for your career, but you're a woman who needs to be loved." He leaned closer and his voice became a whisper, intimate and caressing. "I can give you what you need. You know I can. Don't you remember what it was like with us?"

From beneath his deep fringe of lashes his eyes met hers searchingly. The memories that had haunted Ava for the past five years unfurled inside her, adding to her confusion.

"It can be like that again, Ava," he promised, sliding his hand from the bar to her shoulder. He lowered his head, his lips parting as they sought hers.

"No, don't!" She pushed against his chest with such force she sent him sliding off the edge of the bed. Only his superb agility kept him from falling to the floor, but he was sufficiently off-balance to allow her to get by him. Before he could recover, she'd rushed over to the open doorway. She had to lean against the doorjamb because her legs were trembling. "Don't you ever try that again, Derek," she warned him shakily.

With cool deliberateness he retrieved his cigarettes and lighter before walking over to her. "You can keep me from kissing you now, Ava, but you won't be able to stop me during the love scene." His tone was intimate again, seductive, and he looked deep into her eyes. "Do you still remember the first time we made love?"

He smiled when she dragged her eyes away, as though she'd given him the answer he was hoping for. "I thought you'd like to know I'm going to be using that memory when we do the love scene. Just as I know you will be, too." With his finger, he traced the line of her jaw, then lifted her chin, bringing her eyes back to his. "So remember, when I'm making love to you in a little while, it's not going to be acting."

"That's all it's going to be on my part, Derek," Ava insisted, but her voice was in shreds.

He flashed her a brilliant, supremely confident smile. "We'll see." Turning, he walked out the door.

Ava let out a long, ragged sigh. Why wasn't Kirk here? she wondered angrily.

Nine

Kirk cast a quick glance around the projection room, even though he knew that everyone vitally involved with the rushes was already there. The director and the first A.D. were seated three rows ahead of him; the cinematographer and his first assistant were seated a couple of rows beyond them. Both assistants balanced legal pads on their laps, their pen lights poised to take notes.

Except for Ava, who never attended the daily screenings of the scenes that had been shot the previous day, all the leads in the movie were present that evening. Mike never missed the rushes, taking an even greater interest in his daughter's scenes than his own. He was sitting in his usual aisle seat, huddling with Larry Davenport, who played Francesca's husband in the film. Derek, his long legs stretched out in front of him, was lounging, typically, first row center.

Kirk caught the questioning look Hal was sending him over his shoulder, yet he hesitated to give the projectionist the order to run the rough footage of the love scene. He told himself that although he'd been unable to watch in person as Ava and Derek recreated the passion they'd once shared, seeing it on the screen should have an emotionally distancing effect. He could be objective about it. It was just another scene from a movie.

Still, he hesitated. He knew he was about to get the answer to the question that had haunted him for the past month and made his trip to Rome sheer misery. Was Ava still in love with Derek?

"Is everything all right, Kirk?" asked Hal.

Tilting his head back, Kirk called out. "Are you all set back there, Glenn?"

The projectionist's disembodied voice floated through the square opening in the back wall, "All set."

"Let's run it," Kirk ordered tightly, clutching his pen light as if it were the only thing he had left to hang on to.

The screening room was plunged into darkness; the lit tips of the pens seemed to hang suspended in space like tiny stars in an immense black void. Then the screen flickered alive. Kirk's breath caught when Ava's image flashed on the screen. She was, literally, breathtakingly beautiful.

The burgundy velvet gown she wore clung to every lushly feminine curve of her body, contrasting dramatically with the porcelain tone of her skin and the blue-black sheen of her hair. Desire stirred in him just at the sight of her. The camera was as much in love with her as he was, catching every nuance of feeling on her exquisitely sensitive face, every shift of emotion glowing in the depths of her emerald eyes.

Derek moved into the frame for the two-shot and something wrenched inside Kirk. Derek's beauty and charisma were as unique as Ava's. They looked so perfect together they might have been created with each other in mind. Impotently he watched as they came together in a passionate embrace, the love they could no longer deny lighting up the screen, spilling beyond the boundaries of film.

Kirk was intensely aware of the stunned silence in the room. No notes were being taken as the pen lights remained suspended in midair. Everyone's attention was riveted on the screen. As professionals they were quick to recognize that special magic, which happened so rarely in films, when fantasy fused with reality, catching the performers completely in its spell and dragging the audience along with them.

With growing despair, Kirk watched his most dreaded fear come true. He was positive the rest of them also knew that what they were witnessing went beyond mere artistry—Ava and Derek weren't acting. Love, so real it was almost palpable, was evident in their every look and gesture, in the joy they so obviously found in each other.

He cursed himself for taking the chance and leaving Ava alone with Derek. He'd known that would force her to confront her feelings for her ex-lover once and for all. Now he wondered whether Ava and Derek had taken advantage of his absence to finish the love scene in private.

The camera zoomed in on a tight close-up of Ava, capturing her reaction to Derek's long, ardent kiss. Her face was transfigured by the look of love suffusing it, and Kirk could barely breathe from the pain twisting inside him. He'd have sold his soul on the spot to have her look at him that way just once.

He couldn't watch anymore.

Pride was the only thing keeping him in his seat. He refused to let his emotions get the better of him in front of the others—especially Derek. Blindly he stared at the legal pad on his lap. He couldn't see Ava, but he could still hear her voice, breathless from Derek's kisses, murmuring words of love he'd never heard from her. Words, he knew now, he would never hear from her.

Before he could stop himself, Kirk was out of his chair and tearing down the aisle, gasps of amazement coming at him from both sides. Through the tears stinging his eyes, he caught the smirk of satisfaction on Derek's face.

The phone rang eight times, then, just as Ava was about to hang up, was answered with a stream of colorful and untranslatable Italian curses. Its owner clearly resented being dragged out of bed at that hour of the morning.

"Marco, I'm sorry to wake you," Ava said sincerely, "but it's important."

"Miss Kendall?" Marco said, sounding suddenly wide-awake. "*Scusi*, I did not mean to say such bad things. I did not know it was you."

"I'm the one who should apologize for disturbing you, Marco," she reassured him, "but it's almost two in the morning and Kirk still isn't home. I was hoping you might know where he is."

"*Ma, no.* I left Signor Kirk in Rimini as he requested," Marco told her. "He said for me to take the rest of the evening off and he would drive home himself."

"What time was that?"

"Oh, early." There was a pause at his end of the line while he calculated the exact time. "At dinnertime. Eight o'clock."

"That's when he told me he'd be home, right after they finished screening the rushes." Ava took a long, steadying breath. "Where could he be?"

"*Non so.* He seem to me very... how you say?" There was another searching pause. "Very emotional."

"Emotional? You mean, he was upset?"

"*Si,* upset. Very upset."

"Why? What happened?"

"I cannot say, Miss Kendall. Perhaps some problem with the film?" he suggested in an attempt to be helpful. "Or perhaps Signor Kirk needed to work more with Signor Hal, and they work so late he remain to sleep at the hotel?"

"No, I've already called Hal. He hasn't seen or heard from Kirk all night either."

"Ah, *mi dispiace,*" Marco said with a heartfelt sigh. "I am sorry, Miss Kendall, I cannot be of help to you."

"Thanks, anyway, Marco," Ava murmured. "Go back to sleep. I'm sorry I woke you."

Ava's hand was unsteady when she replaced the antique phone on its hook. The information Marco had just given her only added to her concern. What on earth had possessed Kirk to drive at night on roads he was unfamiliar with? Maybe he'd gotten lost or the car had broken down or...

She felt the blood drain from her face. The steep, winding mountain road leading to the villa might have been a miracle of engineering when the Romans built it a few thousand years ago, but it hadn't been built with stretch limousines in mind. What if he'd had an accident?

"Oh, my God," she murmured brokenly. The premonition she'd been unable to shake all evening gripped her once again—something terrible had happened. Hurrying over to the glass door, she pulled it open and stepped out onto the balcony.

The stone balcony ran the length of the back wall of the villa. As Ava rushed past Kirk's bedroom, she assured herself that he was an excellent driver, as in control behind the wheel as he was in all things. Some production problem must have detained him. But wouldn't Hal have known about it? And surely, Kirk would have called her. He'd promised her he'd come home right after he'd viewed the rushes....

But that was only because she'd insisted, Ava recalled.

She'd managed to hide her disappointment, but not her annoyance, when he'd told her he intended to work late, even though she hadn't seen him for three days. His manner toward her since he'd come back from his trip to Rome had been distant, almost guarded. Still, it wasn't like him to renege on a promise. No matter how busy he was, he always kept his appointments, and he was always on time. Kirk was nothing if not dependable. It was *because* she knew she could depend on him totally that she was worried about him now.

Having reached the end of the balcony, Ava stepped up onto the base of two of the long row of stone columns that provided a protective barrier against the steep plunge to the rocks below. Gripping the rounded edge, she pulled herself up over the top of the balcony, her torso dangling in space as she sought to see around the corner of the building.

The road that wound up from the sea past the front of the villa was barely visible in the darkness and most of it was hidden from her view. Not a single pair of headlights gleamed on the visible stretch of road.

Her arms began to shake from the effort it took to stay balanced in space. With a reluctant sigh, she slid down and turned to walk back to her bedroom. A strange feeling stopped her, held her frozen to the spot. She felt as though the only security she'd ever known had been snatched away from her, leaving her vulnerable and defenseless. Her first impulse was to deny the feeling, to find something external for her mind to latch on to.

A half-moon hung in the dark sky, so perfectly divided someone might have drawn a line down its center with a ruler. But Ava found that she couldn't escape into her fantasies as she used to. All she could think of was Kirk. And as she stared down at the vastness of the sea, she didn't try to lose herself in its beauty or the soothing murmur of its voice. Instead she deliberately recalled the hours she'd spent on the beach yesterday, just walking and thinking.

She'd been trying to figure out why Kirk had stayed on in Rome over the weekend. She'd learned enough about the uniquely Italian way of doing things in the past month to know that he couldn't possibly have been transacting any business on a Sunday. So what could he be doing in Rome all by himself?

Maybe he wasn't by himself, she'd concluded. Perhaps he'd given up on waiting for her to make the first move and had found another woman to satisfy his sexual needs. She'd been surprised to find how much that possibility hurt her. She finally had to admit that she missed him more than she would ever have believed possible.

Yet a part of her had been glad for the chance to be on her own Sunday. She hadn't let anyone know where she was, not even Mike or Derek. She needed to think through the emotions she'd been floundering in. As she walked for hours along the fine sand, with only the sea gulls and the soft murmur of the waves for company, the pine-scented breeze dispersing the autumn fog seemed to clear her mind, as well.

For the first time, she began to see her way clear of the tangle of emotions that bound her to both Kirk and Derek, to both the past and the present. Doing the love scene with

Derek had forced her to finally deal with her feelings for him. She resolved that she and Kirk would have to have a long talk.

But where was he?

Fear and uncertainty gripped Ava again, but she refused to give in to her feelings. If she could just think it through, she was sure she'd be able to understand Kirk's behavior, also.

A gust of wind went up, shaking the branches of the pine trees clinging tenaciously to the sides of the cliffs, scattering the clouds overhead. In spite of the sudden chill, Ava rested her elbows on top of the balcony, and cupping her face in her hands, she stared thoughtfully down at the sea. Word by word, she went over the phone conversation with Marco.

Four of those words stuck in her mind: "*Si,* upset. Very upset."

It wasn't like Kirk to let things affect him emotionally, or if they did, to show it. What could have upset him so much even Marco had been aware of it? Kirk had never seemed more self-possessed when she'd last seen him. Something must have happened since then.

Suddenly the realization struck her, causing her to straighten up again. The rushes! Kirk had just seen the rushes of the love scene. Was it possible that he was jealous? Might he be in love with her, after all? Or was it just an ego—

A rectangle of light spilled over Ava, shattering her thoughts. She spun around. When she saw that it was the light streaming through the glass door of Kirk's bedroom, a gasp of relief tore out of her. Quickly she stepped over to the door and knocked on one of the glass panes.

Within moments the door was opened and Kirk stepped outside. "What are you doing out here?" He seemed anything but pleased to see her as he stood there glaring down at her. "Don't you know what time it is?"

"Where have you been?" Ava cried. "I was afraid something terrible had happened to you."

Something terrible had happened to him. A sarcastic smile twisted his mouth. "Your concern is truly touching."

"Are you all right?" she asked, not allowing his sarcasm to make her withdraw into herself as it usually did. "Has something happened?"

"*I'm* the one who should be asking *you* that."

It suddenly occurred to Ava that Kirk's every response to her lately was loaded with sarcasm. He'd never been that way before. She couldn't remember the last time she'd seen him smile.

"Has anything happened in my absence that I should know about?"

"I don't understand why you did this," Ava persisted, refusing to let him change the subject. "Whatever possessed you to drive at—"

"How do you know I was driving?"

His words sounded a bit slurred and Ava realized that he'd been drinking—heavily. That wasn't like Kirk, either.

"Marco told me."

"You spoke to Marco? When?"

"When I saw how late it was and you still hadn't come home as you'd promised," she explained anxiously. "I didn't know where you were or what had happened to you, so I called Marco...Hal, too. But they didn't know where you were, either."

He raked an impatient hand through his steel-gray hair. "I just felt like taking a long drive. I needed to be alone so I could think."

"But you knew I was waiting for you. I've been waiting for you since nine o'clock. It's after two," she snapped, anger at the hours of worry he'd caused her overriding her sense of relief now that she knew he was safe. "There's a phone in the car. The least you could have done was call me. I am your wife!"

"My wife? Since when have you been a wife to me?"

The lacerating bitterness of his words cut right through Ava, leaving her speechless. She saw pain in the rugged lines of his face, and in the depths of his eyes. Had she done that to him?

She took a step toward him. "Kirk, I've been doing a lot of thinking too these past few days."

"I'll bet you have," Kirk muttered, his voice hard. The pity he saw on her face was the last thing he wanted from her. The close-up of her face transfigured with love for Derek still burned behind his eyes. No matter how fast or how far he drove or how many drinks he had, he'd been unable to wipe that image out of his consciousness.

"Please," she insisted, "I have to talk to you."

Kirk stiffened against the impact of the words he was sure she was going to say next. "Don't bother," he grated, not giving her the chance to say them. He couldn't bear to hear them. "I already know what you have to say to me."

"We can't go on this way, Kirk," Ava protested, determined to talk things out between them at last. "We have to—"

"You're right. We can't go on this way," he cut her off savagely. "So why don't we just admit this marriage was a mistake from the beginning. I don't know how in hell I managed to delude myself that it could possibly work." He stepped back into his room. "You can have a divorce, Ava, on any terms you want," he added, his voice raw. "Let's just get this over with!"

The glass panes rattled dangerously when he slammed the door in her face. It was the only way he could defend himself against her, against how much he still wanted her.

They both stood there for a long moment on either side of the door, still visible to each other through the sheer drapes. And then Ava turned and walked slowly back to her room.

It wasn't Ava's usual actor's nightmare of being stuck onstage in the wrong play with the wrong lines. The feeling of being emotionally naked was the same, as was the audience's hostile ridicule, but she was sure there was a way out for her this time. Kirk would know what it was. If only she could find him.

Reciting the only lines she knew, even though she knew they were the wrong ones, she searched frantically for him in the wings. He wasn't there. But her father was. Mike was prompting her from the enormous script he was holding, giving her the lines she should have been speaking, but the lines were in Italian.

She suddenly realized that she was in modern dress, while everyone else onstage was in costume. The catcalls from the audience were getting longer and louder. Derek, who was playing Romeo to her Juliet, had to raise his voice to give her her cue. She was amazed that he spoke Italian so perfectly.

The sound of someone hammering added to her confusion. When she looked upstage, she saw that the set was only half finished. The carpenter was still nailing canvas to the missing flat that should have been the back wall of the castle. She knew Kirk would never have permitted him to do that in the middle of a performance—but where was he?

The sound of hammering was getting louder, so loud—

So loud it woke her up.

It took Ava a moment to realize that she'd been dreaming and that the hammering was actually someone knocking on her bedroom door.

"*Scusi*, Signora Ava," Marina apologized as she let herself in, balancing the breakfast tray with one hand. "But it is nine o'clock."

"Nine o'clock!" Ava threw off the covers and jumped out of bed. "Why didn't I get my wake-up call at seven?"

"Signor Kirk told me to permit you to sleep longer this morning," Marina explained as she carried the tray over to the dining alcove. Besides the silver carafes of coffee and warm milk, it held a plate overflowing with fresh rolls and croissants. Marina still hadn't given up on getting Ava to eat breakfast. "He is having a meeting with several *signori* downstairs."

"A meeting . . . here at the house?" Ava sent Marina an incredulous look. Kirk never conducted business at the house. "What kind of a meeting?"

"Ah, *non so*. I know only that he has been on the telephone since seven o'clock." Carefully she set the silver tray down on the table. "And then when Marco arrived, he sent him to Rimini to bring the *signori* here."

Ava paused as she was about to slip into her robe. She recalled the last words Kirk had spoken to her: *"You can have a divorce, Ava . . . let's just get this over with!"*

"Lawyers?" she murmured. Was that why Kirk had set up this meeting, to draw up the necessary papers for a divorce?

"Lawyers?" repeated Marina. Only then did Ava realize she'd spoken aloud.

"Si, è possible," Marina added thoughtfully when she'd finished preparing the *caffelatte*. "When I served them breakfast they all had the faces of lawyers." With her ex-

pressive hand, she made a gesture indicating a long face. "Very serious, they were, as when they're reading the last will."

"I'd better take my shower now," Ava said tightly.

"Everything is all right, I hope, Signora Ava?"

Marina's genuine concern made it impossible for Ava to lie to her. "I'm afraid not, Marina."

"Signor Kirk, he has not been himself of late."

"No, he hasn't," Ava admitted. And it was all her fault. She turned away so Marina wouldn't see how upset she was. "It's getting late. I'd better start getting dressed."

"Can I be of assistance?"

"No, thank you, Marina." Ava slanted her what she hoped was a cheerful smile.

It didn't seem to reassure her. *"Amore,"* she muttered under her breath. With a heavy sigh and much fatalistic shaking of her head, Marina crossed over to the door. *"Caffelatte* is not good when it is cold," she grumbled over her shoulder before she closed the door behind her.

Ava had to force herself to move. She showered and dressed on automatic pilot. As she was searching through the top drawer of her dresser for the belt that went with the denim jumpsuit she was wearing, she stumbled across the jewelry box she'd tucked inside the drawer weeks ago.

She'd meant to return the emerald pendant to Kirk, but she'd gotten so caught up in everything she'd forgotten all about it. She would certainly have to return his extravagant gift to him now. Without opening the slender velvet box, she slipped it into one of the zippered pockets of her jumpsuit. Pausing only to grab her bag, she walked quickly out of the bedroom and down the stairs to the first floor.

Her steps slowed when she approached the dining room as the sound of male voices drifted through the open door. Though she couldn't make out the words, it seemed to her that the conversation had a distinctly legal tone to it. She came to a tense halt in the doorway.

A great feeling of relief flooded her when she recognized the men seated around the table with Kirk. Hal had just finished making a point that "Dutch," the cinematographer, obviously agreed with. Kirk's right-hand man, associate producer Alex Elliot, was busy taking notes.

Kirk was seated with his back to the door, so Ava couldn't see his face. His uneaten breakfast had been pushed to the center of the table; in its place was an open folder filled with charts and schedules.

Hal was about to make another point, when he caught sight of Ava in the doorway.

"I'm sorry to interrupt," Ava told everyone, continuing into the dining room.

Kirk stiffened visibly at the sound of her voice. Slowly he turned to look over at her.

Ava was shocked by his appearance. He was still wearing the suit he'd come home in last night, so she assumed he hadn't gone to bed at all. The collar of his shirt was unbuttoned and his tie hung like a crooked silk noose halfway down his chest. His usually perfectly groomed hair looked as if it had been combed with impatient fingers; a salt-and-pepper stubble covered the rugged line of his jaw.

He looked exhausted. It hurt her to see him that way.

She wanted to ask him how he was, to say something to relieve the tension tightening his strong, rough features, narrowing his eyes, but she held back. The reason for his appearance, she knew, was not something they could discuss in front of the others.

Kirk turned back to his charts and schedules. "That's all right, Ava," he said coolly. "We were just rehashing a few details while we waited for you to get ready. We've already taken care of everything we had to." Shutting the folder, he handed it across the table to the associate producer. "You all know what has to be done now, gentlemen, am I right?"

While everyone voiced his agreement, Ava silently cursed herself for a fool. She should have known the only problem serious enough to keep Kirk up all night would have to do with his work.

"We still have a movie to finish," he reminded them all as he reached for his cup of black coffee.

Chairs screeched against the polished wood floor as everyone jumped to his feet—everyone except Kirk. When Ava realized he had no intention of joining them, she asked, "Aren't you coming to the set with us?"

"No," he told her without so much as a glance in her direction. "I still have a few things to take care of." He turned toward the associate producer. "Alex, as you're passing the foyer, would you please tell Signor Lombardi I can see him now."

"Certainly, Kirk," Alex agreed.

Signor Lombardi had what Marina would have called the face of a lawyer, Ava noted, when she passed the ultraconservatively dressed gentleman seated stiffly on a marble bench in the foyer. As she watched him walk toward the dining room, a leather attaché case clutched firmly in one hand, she wondered whether he was a corporate lawyer or a divorce lawyer.

Ten

Ava had never found silence so oppressive. It was the kind of embarrassed silence that sometimes occurred at funerals when people didn't quite know what to say to the bereaved. Throughout the drive to the castle all three men made a determined show of studying the notes they'd written during their meeting with Kirk. Hal slid her an occasional smile of sympathy, which only added to her feeling that someone in her family had died.

She was grateful for the noise and confusion that greeted them when they arrived on the set. The electrical crew was busy stringing lights, while the grips were laying dolly tracks, which the camera would use to glide on for traveling shots or to dolly toward or away from the action. Orders from the heads of the crews, and their subsequent translations, had to be shouted in order to be heard above the pandemonium, which of course, only added to it.

Looking even more hassled than usual, the A.D., quickly wended his way through the tangle of men and equipment. "Thank God, you're here," he told Hal when he reached them. "You wouldn't believe what's been going on this morning."

"What seems to be the problem?" Hal inquired in his typically unflappable manner. "Didn't you get the first setup in the can?"

"We haven't even started shooting the first setup! That guy Rossi's been giving us more trouble!" The A.D. looked around frantically. "Where's Kirk? He's the only one who can handle that guy."

Alex, the associate producer, stepped forward. "I'll take care of it. Where is Signor Rossi?"

"He's over there arguing with the key grip," Barry muttered with a disgusted wave of his arm. "You'd think we were trying to lay dolly tracks in the Vatican, for God's sake!"

"I'll talk to him," Alex said reassuringly. Tucking the folder Kirk had given him under one arm, he started toward the curator of the castle, while "Dutch" went in search of his first cameraman.

"Seems we're in for another wonderful day in the wonderful land of Oz," Hal drawled wryly before turning his attention to Ava, who was beginning to feel just a bit overwhelmed. "It looks to me like it's going to take a couple of hours before we get this mess straightened out. Why don't you go and lie down in your dressing room? You look very tired."

"Yes, I am." She hadn't gotten more than four hours' sleep and she felt emotionally as well as physically drained from the events of the previous night. "Are you sure it's all right?"

"That's an order," the director told her firmly but gently. "And put the *Do Not Disturb* sign on your door. I'll send Barry to tell you when you can get into makeup and costume."

"Thanks, Hal," Ava said gratefully.

He gave her another one of those smiles of sympathy he'd given her in the car, which only made her feel worse. Somehow she couldn't shake the feeling that Hal knew something she didn't—something about Kirk.

Before she could ask him about it, the director's attention had turned to the more immediate problem of getting everything ready so he could start shooting. Suddenly all the noise and confusion on the set began grating on Ava's already strained nerves. She longed for the quiet of her dressing room, and the chance to pull herself together.

But when Ava reached her dressing room, she found Makeup waiting there for her.

"Hey, what's wrong?" Cathy asked as she looked up from the afghan she always knitted in her spare time. "You're so pale. Are you feeling okay?"

"Yes, I'm fine," Ava said, forcing a reassuring smile. "Just a bit tired."

"How come you're so late?"

"Kirk had a meeting first thing this morning and—"

"Here you are—finally!" Derek exclaimed as he came rushing in from his dressing room next door, a disgruntled Leon on his heels. He was already in makeup and wearing a fitted brocade tunic and tights. "I knew I heard your voice."

"I haven't finished doing your curly locks, handsome," Leon reminded him, a spiral brush in one hand, a cordless curling iron in the other. "Would you be so kind as to get back in your..."

He forgot to finish his sentence when he caught sight of Ava. "What on earth happened to you, lovely? You look like you could play Camille without makeup." He sent Cathy a look of heartfelt commiseration. "You're going to have your work cut out for you today, Red."

"She doesn't look that bad," Cathy said in Ava's defense. "I've seen worse in my—"

"Would you two mind talking shop somewhere else?" Derek cut in impatiently. "I'd like to speak to Ava alone for a—"

"Please, everybody," Ava interrupted for a change, "just stop it!"

They all turned and looked at her in stunned silence. It was the first time she'd ever raised her voice on the set or made a demand of any kind.

"May I say something for once?" She took a long, steadying breath. Making demands was so new to her she almost didn't know where to begin. "Hal just told me that they won't be ready to shoot for a couple of hours, so I'd like to lie down for a while. He'll let us know when they're ready."

"Strange things are happening," Leon drawled. "What's going on?" He looked from Ava to Derek as though he were sure only they knew the answer. "Rumors are rife."

"Rumors?" Ava asked. "What kind of rumors?"

Cathy looked down at her afghan. Leon looked at Derek. Derek smiled.

"What kind of rumors?"

"Just . . . rumors," Derek said, his tone rich with innuendo, his smile embarrassingly intimate.

"Well, I'm not interested in hearing them." Turning away from the others, Ava stepped over to the door to get the *Do not Disturb* sign. "All I'm interested in is taking a nap so I'll be able to work later."

"You certainly look like you can use a nap, lovely," Leon agreed when he saw the sign she was holding. He slanted another knowing glance in Derek's direction. "Come on, Red," he urged, "let's go get another cup of that simply devastating Italian coffee."

"If I have another cup of coffee this..." Cathy began. "Oh, sure," she was quick to add, as if she'd just gotten Leon's meaning. Gathering up her afghan and her knitting bag, she jumped to her feet. "I guess I could go for another cup of coffee."

Her hand suspended in midair, Ava stared at the two of them as they hurried past her and out the door.

"Now that's a good idea," Derek said. Sliding his index finger under the cord, he lifted the sign out of her hand. "I didn't know how I'd manage to see you alone today. Your father's already been down here twice looking for you." He slipped the sign over the outside door handle ever so casually. "But where's Kirk? I heard he's not here again today. Is that true?"

"Yes," Ava was forced to admit. "He's been detained. He had a very important meeting."

"Doesn't he always?" he said pointedly, closing the door behind him.

"Derek, I told you, I want to take a nap."

"But I've got to talk to you," he insisted. "You went out of your way to avoid me all weekend, the least—"

"Please, not now!" She was already upset about Kirk's "meeting." The last thing she needed was to have to deal with Derek. Brushing past him, she reached for the door handle.

"But I've got to tell you about the rushes!"

"The rushes?" Ava's hand slid off the handle and she turned back to him.

"God, I wish you'd been there," he said, his eyes glowing. "Why weren't you there?"

"I never go to the rushes," she reminded him. "I don't like seeing myself. It makes me too self-conscious."

"But you were terrific!"

She dismissed the compliment with an impatient wave of her hand. "Tell me what happened."

"Remember what it's like when you're onstage on a really good night? Everything's working for you. You can't do anything wrong. Suddenly there isn't a sound from the audience." He paused and stood perfectly still, commanding attention by the sheer magnetism of his presence, and with only the evocative power of his voice, he made the experience come alive. "Not a whisper. Not one cough. All of them holding their breaths, watching and waiting to see what you're going to do next." He clenched his hand dramatically. "That's when you know you've hooked them."

He turned to her, including her in his performance. "Well, that's exactly what happened during the screening of our love scene last night." He shook his fist triumphantly. "A roomful of pros who've seen it all, and we hooked them!"

"That's not what I meant, Derek. I—"

"What we had going between us was so strong, Ava," he went on, too caught up in the experience to be able to stop, "it just jumped right off the screen and grabbed everybody. You should have seen their reactions!"

"What was Kirk's reaction?"

Remembering brought a slow smile to his lips. "Let me put it this way, he didn't exactly look overjoyed. But what man *would* be, watching his wife expressing her love for another man?"

"That was a scene in a movie, Derek," Ava protested. "I was only acting."

"Neither one of us was acting, Ava, and you know it," he tossed back with great satisfaction. "And so does everyone who saw that scene. Your feelings for me were real."

"Of course my feelings were real," she countered. "I was doing an 'emotion memory' of the first time we...I made love. I would have done the same with any actor who played Paolo."

"Is that what you told Kirk?" From beneath his long lashes he slid her a wry look. "I'm willing to bet he didn't buy that, either." He took a step toward her. "What did he say about it?"

Ava shook her head slowly. "Nothing."

"Nothing?" He sounded disappointed. "The way he looked when he left I thought for sure you two were going to have a major fight."

"How did he look?" she asked with more emotion than she'd intended. "Was he very upset?"

"Well, I'm not sure 'upset' is the right choice of words," he said evasively. "I don't have to tell you what Kirk's like. He's used to getting his own way in everything, and he doesn't like it one damn bit when he doesn't." He laughed scornfully. "Kirk Falconer always gets what he wants. Isn't that what he's famous for?"

Ava wished she could argue the point, but no one knew better than she that Derek was right. What she'd hoped had been jealousy on Kirk's part, she realized, had been merely hurt pride.

"I wonder what he's planning to do now?" Derek said thoughtfully. "I'm sure he's not going to throw me off the picture. Not with a month's worth of film already in the can.'' His air of confidence seemed a bit forced. ''He'd have to reshoot everything.''

''Even if he had only *one* day's worth of film in the can,'' Ava said, suddenly on the defensive, ''Kirk wouldn't fire you for personal reasons. He's not like that.'' Turning, she walked away from him.

''So what's he going to do?'' When she didn't, couldn't, answer, he followed her over to the makeup table. ''Did he say?'' Studying her reflection in the mirror, he caught the look of pain that flashed in her eyes. ''He obviously told you something.''

''Yes,'' she admitted, turning back to him. There was really no point in concealing the truth from him, since everyone involved with the production would hear about it soon enough. ''He's going to get a divorce.''

''A divorce?'' Derek clearly hadn't anticipated that particular piece of news, and it took him a moment to recover. ''Well, *that's* certainly not like Kirk. I wouldn't have expected him to give up so easily.''

''No,'' Ava murmured under her breath, ''neither would I.''

Suddenly Derek's face lit up, his brilliant blue eyes glowing as though he'd just been nominated for an Academy Award. ''Then he's willing to set you free! That's great!''

''Is it? I'm glad you think so.''

He shrugged off her sarcasm. ''Come on, Ava, you know you don't love Kirk.''

''No, of course not,'' she agreed, her tone brittle. Then why did she feel such a deep, aching sense of loss?

''And Kirk doesn't need you. He doesn't need anybody. He's got his work.'' He must have sensed how vulnerable she was at that moment, because he took her softly by the shoulders. "But I do need you, Ava. I always have. I know that now." A rueful smile flickered over his beautiful face. "God, what a fool I was. I should have married you years ago. You're the only woman I've ever loved."

Ava couldn't help but admire Derek's technique. The catch in his voice was very effective, she thought. She couldn't resist asking, "So, to quote an old Hollywood cliché, you were 'just good friends' with all those other women?"

"Not one of those women ever meant anything to me," he assured her, his tone as seductive as the expensive men's cologne that assailed her as he drew her close. "Only you."

The irony of the situation she found herself in was not entirely lost on Ava. She was emotionally caught between two men; one who was incapable of saying I love you and the other who said it too easily.

She suddenly felt very tired. "Leave me alone, Derek." She placed her hands on his chest to push him away. "I've got to take a nap now or—"

"Don't you realize what I'm saying, you little fool?" He shook her lightly as if to shake some sense into her. "I'm asking you to marry me."

"What?"

"Now do you believe I love you?"

She was too astonished to reply. She let her hands slide off his chest and fall to her sides.

"Well, say something," he cried, throwing his hands up in mock despair. "The suspense is killing me."

Ava felt as if her whole world had been turned upside down twice in one day. Barely realizing it, she walked over to the daybed and sank slowly down onto the mattress.

"Look, I know I don't have the money and power Kirk has," Derek went on, coming over to her, "but once this movie is released I'm going to be right back on top again. Everyone says so."

"I didn't love you because you were famous, Derek," she reminded him. "You weren't then."

"I know that. You're the only one who's ever loved me for myself." He sat down on the daybed next to her. "That's why I need you, Ava. I never realized how much I needed you until I saw the rushes last night."

"The rushes?" she murmured uncomprehendingly.

"God, I wish you could have seen them. It's the best work I've done in years." He flashed her a grateful and rather touching smile. "But I couldn't have done it without you."

"That's not true," she told him sincerely. "You're a very talented actor."

"Talent isn't enough. Success isn't, either. I'm sure I'd just blow it all away again without you." Reaching over, he took one of her hands in his. "You'll never know how much you've done for me. *You're* the only reason I've been able to stay sober this past month." Lifting her hand to his lips, he kissed it tenderly. From beneath his long, thick lashes he gave her a look guaranteed to melt the hardest heart. "You've got to marry me, Ava. Don't you see how much I need you?"

"But, Derek—"

He placed his index finger against her lips, silencing her. "Say no more. I know what you're waiting for." He flashed her a mischievous grin. "A formal proposal. And you shall have it."

As he went down on one knee before her, he squinted his eyes and drew his dark brows together in an uncanny imitation of Clark Gable. "Forgive me for startling you with the impetuosity of my proposal, my dear Scarlett, but it cannot have escaped your notice that for some time now—''

Ava burst out laughing in spite of herself, making Derek laugh also.

''I was beginning to think I'd lost my touch,'' he said when he sat down beside her again. ''But I'm glad to see I can still make you laugh.'' His eyes met hers; a world of memories gleamed in them. ''We did have a lot of fun together, didn't we?''

''Yes,'' Ava was forced to admit, ''we did.'' She had to swallow past the lump in her throat. She couldn't believe she'd ever been that young and carefree. ''But that was five years ago, Derek. A lot has happened since then.''

''What do I have to say to get you to marry me?'' he pleaded with an absolutely heartbreaking smile. ''Then we can finally forget the past five years ever happened.''

But the past five years *had* happened.

For five long years Ava had lived this moment in her fantasies. On countless lonely nights, unable to fall asleep, she'd imagined Derek pleading for her forgiveness, assuring her he loved her more than before, begging her to marry him—just as he was doing now. The words he was saying were almost the same; she might have written them for him herself. The emotion in his voice and suffusing his face was almost identical. Only her feelings were different.

In her fantasies she'd always been ecstatically happy. Yet now all she felt was a kind of dazed detachment.

Suddenly Ava understood why Derek had filled her fantasies for years, making it impossible for her to let go her love for him. He was practically irresistible. With his perfectly beautiful face and body, his undeniable charm, Derek was the embodiment of every woman's fantasies.

The romantic lover they all dreamed of but rarely found in reality.

He was Prince Charming!

"Ava, are you listening to me?" Derek was asking somewhat impatiently, unaccustomed to a detached audience.

"Yes . . . yes, of course."

"Then why didn't you answer my question?" He let out a sigh of frustration. There was something immensely appealing about the "lost little boy" look in his eyes. "Why won't you marry me? Isn't that what you'd always wanted?"

She nodded. "Yes, it was what I'd always wanted."

"You can't deny you still love me," he insisted, "because I saw how much you love me last night. Everyone saw it. It jumped right off the screen!"

"Derek, I told you, I was just acting."

He looked at her as though she'd read her line out of character, forcing him to make an adjustment in his.

"Okay," he said finally with a disarming grin, "we're not in front of the cameras now. Let's find out, once and for all, whether you still love me."

Derek slipped his arm around her waist. He hesitated as he was about to draw her over to him, as if he expected her to protest. But Ava had no intention of protesting. She was as eager as he to finally find the answer to that question— maybe more. She had a lot more at stake.

He placed his other arm confidently around her shoulders, supporting the weight of her body when he dipped her back, draping her across the cushions with a motion so fluid it might have been choreographed. Tilting his head, he brought his lips down to hers at a perfect angle.

His mouth moving on hers expertly, exquisitely, Derek kissed her the way every woman dreams of being kissed. And Ava finally had her answer.

Having given up on being able to take a nap after her encounter with Derek, Ava went upstairs. The noise and confusion that had greeted her earlier had settled down to a controlled pandemonium. The gaffer was positioning the last of the arc lights, while the camera crew was testing the dolly tracks to make sure the camera's movements would be steady and fluid.

As Ava glanced searchingly around the war and council room to see whether Kirk had arrived yet, she was aware of a nervous, almost fearful fluttering in her stomach. But there was no sign of him. Catching sight of her father, she moved toward him thinking he would know where Kirk was.

Mike was pacing up and down in front of the wide fireplace that dominated one wall, muttering to himself in an agitated way. Since she knew they were shooting Mike's big scene that day—the one in which Francesca's father tricks her into a loveless marriage—she assumed he was going over his lines.

He let out an enormous sigh of relief when she stopped beside him. Grabbing her wrist, he turned her around so they were both facing the opening in the fireplace, their backs to the rest of the room. "I've been going out of my mind waiting for you to finish your nap," he stage-whispered.

"Why? What's happened?"

"That's what *I* want to know!" He threw his hands up in frustration. "Since *last* night I've been going out of my mind wondering what happened after Kirk stormed out of the screening room!"

"Kirk *stormed* out of the screening room?"

"Right in the middle of the rushes!"

"In the middle of the rushes?" Ava repeated incredulously again. "In front of everybody?"

"Yes!" He glared at her accusingly. "Does Kirk know you and Derek were once lovers?"

Still recovering from that extraordinary piece of news, Ava managed a vague nod. "I told him myself."

"Oh, my God," he groaned. "Didn't you realize you'd ruin everything? Why did you do such a thing?"

"Because he's my husband. I owed him the truth."

"What about *me*?" he cried loudly, stabbing himself repeatedly in the chest with his index finger. "*I'm* your father, and you owe *me* something too after all the sacrifices I made for you!"

"Mike, please," Ava implored, embarrassed by the intensity of his outburst. Casting a quick glance around the set, she was relieved to see that the members of the crew had taken no notice. Everyone obviously assumed they were just rehearsing their scene.

"How could you do that to me?" he demanded, lowering his tone to a stage whisper again. "Is it true what everyone's saying, that you and Derek are playing love scenes off camera, too?"

"No, of course not!" Ava was shocked and hurt that her father could even consider such a thing possible.

While he turned the implications of her statement over in his mind, she stared at him just as thoughtfully. Since the night Kirk had accused Ava of allowing Mike to exploit her, she had begun seeing things about her father she'd never been aware of before.

"You'd just better make sure Kirk knows there's nothing going on between you and Derek," he ordered, shaking his finger at her as though she were still a child.

"Because after seeing those rushes last night, he's got to think—"

"But Derek *has* told me he still loves me," Ava cut him off defiantly. "And he's asked me to marry him." She found some satisfaction in the look of absolute horror on his face.

"Oh, my God! Don't you realize what that would mean? You'd be destroying your career before it even begins!"

"My career? That's all you really care about, isn't it?" she murmured as the realization spread through her slowly. "My happiness means nothing to you."

"How can you say that? Everything I've ever done was for your happiness," he protested. "When you're rich and famous you'll be happy, princess. Take my word for it."

"No, I'm not going to take your word for it, Mike. Not anymore!"

"Have your forgotten already what it's like to struggle?" he reminded her. "For years we worked and sacrificed to make this dream come true. You can't just throw it away!"

"But it's *your* dream, not mine!" she cried resentfully. "I'm sorry, but I can't make your dreams come true, only you can, and you've got to stop expecting me to!"

He stared at her in total shock for a moment. It was the first time she'd ever raised her voice to him. "I don't understand, I...I always thought we had the same dream."

"I thought so, too," Ava admitted sadly. "But I know now that it was always your dream, Mike. I just went along with it to please you, to make it up to you for all the disappointments you'd..." Her voice caught and she had to take a deep breath before she could continue. "I love acting, but I've never cared about being a big star. And I can only stay with Kirk if I love him, not because of my career.''

''But, princess,'' Mike stammered, despair tightening the premature lines on his face.

''*I* have a dream, too, Mike,'' she went on, refusing to give in to the feelings of guilt threatening to overwhelm her as she always had. ''A dream I'd given up on because I didn't believe it would ever come true. But now I'm going to do everything I can to make it come true...if it isn't too late.''

''What dream?'' He sounded as if he'd only just realized that she was a separate person with dreams and needs of her own.

''The kind of dream of love and marriage most women have.'' She gave him a rueful smile. ''My dream may not be as glamorous as yours, Mike, but at least it won't ruin my life the way yours did.''

Tears flooded her father's eyes, and his frail face looked as though it were going to crumble to pieces in front of her.

''I love you, Dad,'' Ava said, tears misting her own eyes. ''And I'll always be grateful for everything you did for me.'' Putting her arm around his thin shoulders, she hugged him to her side. ''I want to give you back as much as I can, but only I can decide what I'm going to do with my life.'' Blinking back the tears, she kissed him softly on the cheek, then stepped back. ''Only I can choose the man I want to love and marry. And I have.''

Shaking his head forlornly, Mike turned away and stared into the fireplace.

''You know, sometimes I wish you'd give me a little more credit,'' she told him. ''You might be surprised. I just might make the right decision.''

But he wasn't listening to her. He dabbed his eyes with his handkerchief and blew his nose loudly. ''So it's true,

then," he said with a defeated sigh. "Because of this...
thing between you and Derek, Kirk has taken himself off
the picture."

"Are you serious?" Ava laughed wryly. "An earth-
quake couldn't get Kirk off this picture."

"I didn't believe it when I heard it, either." Stuffing his
handkerchief back in his pocket, he looked over at her
again. "But that's all anyone's been talking about today.
They say Kirk stepped down and he's appointed Alex Elliot executive producer."

"That's impos—" The image of Kirk handing his
schedule folder to Alex over the dining room table flashed
in Ava's mind. Suddenly all the pieces of the puzzle—the
emergency meeting Kirk had called that morning, the embarrassed silence in the car, Hal's smiles of sympathy—fell
into place, forming a complete picture.

"Where's Hal?" Ava cried. Spinning around, she
searched frantically for him among the tangle of men and
equipment littering the room. Having spotted him huddling over a table with "Dutch," she left her father standing there and went rushing over to him.

"Hal, I must talk to you!"

"What is it, Ava?" the director asked without looking
up from the storyboards he and the cinematographer had
been discussing.

"It's urgent." The uncharacteristic demand in her voice
finally got his attention. "It's about Kirk."

"Okay," he agreed in his typically nonchalant way.
Taking her by the elbow, he led her to one side. "What's
the problem?"

"Is it true that Kirk's taken himself off the picture?"

"Sure, didn't you know? He's flying back to the States
this evening."

"What?"

"You mean, he didn't tell you?"

Ava shook her head wildly. "I don't understand. Why would he give up the film? His work is the most important thing in the world to him."

Hal lifted a blasé shoulder. "Did you really think he could stand watching you and Derek doing any more love scenes the way he feels about you?"

Ava's lips parted but she was unable to answer.

"You know, I was glad when Kirk married you. I figured it was about time he found some personal happiness. And I'm really sorry to hear about this breakup." He shrugged fatalistically, like a man who'd seen it all and for whom life held no more surprises. "I guess it's just the nature of the crazy business we're in. Come on, let's get back to work."

"No, I can't." She stepped back. "I've got to see Kirk before he leaves."

A world-weary sigh escaped him. "Leave him alone, Ava. You've hurt him enough."

"Hal, the stories that have been going around about Derek and me aren't true," she insisted. "I can't let Kirk leave believing they are."

The look he gave her made her feel he'd heard that one before, too. "Let's go, Ava. Get into makeup and costume. We're just about ready to shoot your scene."

"I don't care about the scene," Ava cried angrily. "I don't care about the whole damn movie! All I care about is Kirk!"

Hal pulled back in uncharacteristic amazement, then a wide grin spread across his face. "Hey, that's all right," he said with more animation than she'd ever seen from him. "Okay, go on. I'll use your stand-in for the long shots and we'll shoot around you."

"Thanks, Hal."

Hal shook his head as he watched Ava hurrying off—
and he'd thought he'd seen everything.

Eleven

Ava came to an abrupt halt in front of Kirk's bedroom door. Her heart was pounding and she was out of breath from having run up the entire flight of stairs. She'd meant to take a moment to compose herself, but was so anxious to see him and—according to Marco—there was so little time left before his flight, she knocked quickly on the door, instead.

"Come in, Marco," Kirk called out while he stuffed another shirt into the valise lying open on his bed. Without straightening, he slid a glance over his shoulder when he heard the door swing open. "Did you call the airport to verify the—" The rest of the words stuck in his throat when he saw Ava standing in the doorway.

He thought he'd never see her again. He never wanted to see her again. But something quickened inside him at the sight of her. Her face was flushed, her hair spilled wildly down her shoulders and back and her emerald eyes glowed almost feverishly, reminding him of the way she'd looked after he'd made love to her. He could almost feel her body still trembling in his arms.

With a silent curse he tore his gaze away from her. Reaching blindly for another shirt, he shoved it into the valise. "What are you doing here?"

Still struggling to catch her breath, Ava looked around somewhat dazedly. Though it was the first time she'd ever been in Kirk's bedroom she didn't bother taking in the decor, which was opulent yet masculine. When she looked at the massive, intricately carved armoire she noticed only that it had been stripped bare of clothes. The drawers that had been left open in the matching dresser had also been emptied.

The impressive beauty of the large canopied bed, with its quilted satin bedspread that gleamed as golden as the sunlight streaming through the high windows, was also lost on her. Her attention was fixed on the suitcase he was packing, the custom-made shirts strewn over the bed as if they'd just been dumped out of a drawer. A garment bag and a large pullman with wheels had already been packed and were waiting only a few feet away from her beside the door for Marco to collect them.

"It is true—you *are* leaving," she murmured, still unable to believe, in spite of the obvious, that Kirk had chosen to give up his work because of her. She needed to hear him confirm it. "Why are you leaving?"

"I don't want you here, Ava," he told her without looking at her. "Get out."

Kirk's harsh words held Ava frozen in the doorway for a moment. Then she recalled other, softer, words: *"When you're ready to admit that you want me as much as I want you, you'll have to come to me."* She stepped farther into the room and closed the door firmly behind her.

Kirk straightened up like a shot and turned toward her. "What do you want, Ava? Why aren't you on the set?"

"Why aren't you?" she asked pointedly, starting toward him.

He want back to his packing. "The way things are, my presence on the set would only cause more problems," he replied evenly. "A producer's job is to solve problems, not create them."

Ava stopped at the foot of the bed and studied Kirk intently. He was dressed as she'd last seen him, in the shirt and pants he'd worn the previous night. They looked wrinkled now, as though he'd slept in them since. His always carefully groomed hair was a silvery tangle, and he still hadn't shaved. She longed to reach out and smooth away the lines of exhaustion that edged his dark, intense eyes and sensuous mouth.

She grabbed on to one of the end bedposts, instead. "Why didn't you tell me you were leaving, Kirk?"

"I believe it's customary for the husband to vacate the premises when a marriage breaks up," he drawled sarcastically.

"It's also customary for a couple to try to work out their problems," Ava pointed out, "or at least discuss them. I never said I wanted a divorce."

He laughed once, harshly. "No, you just said if you'd had a choice you never would have married me in the first place."

"That's true, I did say that," she had to admit. "But it was only because—"

"You don't owe me any explanations, Ava," he interrupted with a weary sigh. "You've always been honest with me. I knew you didn't love me when you married me. I have no right to expect anything from you."

Ava was completely thrown by Kirk's attitude. Accustomed to being emotionally manipulated, first by her father and then by Derek, she'd expected Kirk to put the entire fault for the failure of their marriage on her. She couldn't have blamed him if he had. She realized, more than ever, how wrong all her preconceptions about him had been.

Searchingly she looked up into his eyes. "Did *you* love me when you married me, Kirk?"

He looked away, shrugging evasively. "What's the point in going into all this now?"

"I have to know," she insisted tightly. "Do you love me, Kirk?"

"What do you really want, Ava?" He resumed packing impatiently, almost angrily. "Why are you here?"

"To ask you not to leave." She was still unsure of his feelings for her, and that admission took more courage than she knew she possessed. "And to tell you I'm willing to give our marriage another chance...if you are."

"This is beginning to sound like something your father put you up to. Did Mike have another one of his little talks with you?"

"No, as a matter of fact," she informed him proudly. "This time *I* had a little talk with Mike."

"Oh?" He slid her a bemused glance.

"I finally succeeded in getting him to realize that he can't tell me what to do anymore." She leaned against the bedpost. "And that from now on I intend to make my own choices and decisions."

He smiled crookedly. "I would have loved to have seen that."

"I wish you had," she told him sincerely. "It may have taken me a long time to finally learn to stand up for myself, but I certainly did it with a vengeance. I stood up to my father. I finally settled things with Derek. I'm afraid I even yelled at poor Hal when he wouldn't give me permission to leave the set at first." She laughed. "It's really been quite a day for me. I must remember this date so I can celebrate it every year as my own personal Independence Day."

"So you're here to tell me off, too, is that it?"

She laughed again, softly this time. "I've never had any trouble telling you off, Kirk."

"I'd noticed that," he said wryly, looking over at her.

She held his gaze. "That's because you always encouraged me to express my opinions even when you didn't agree with them. You're the only person who ever has. I really have you to thank for what I did today."

She gave him a smile that went right through him, threatening the defenses he'd so carefully erected against her. "I'm glad you got something out of this marriage," he managed sardonically, tossing the last of the shirts into the valise. "In a little while you'll be free of me, too, and you'll finally be able to—"

"But I don't want to be free of you, Kirk," Ava broke in, coming around the corner of the bed. "That's why I'm here."

"You don't need me anymore, Ava. This film is going to make you a star." With one tug of his powerful hand, he spun the valise around so the empty half was facing him. "Then you'll have everything you ever wanted. Fame. Fortune. And Derek."

"I don't care about being a star. That's Mike's dream, not mine," Ava declared. "And I don't want Derek, I want you!"

He laughed bitterly. "When did you decide that?"

"This weekend when you were in Rome," she admitted, sinking down onto the foot of the bed. "I realized how much I missed you. I couldn't stop thinking about you... about us."

Kirk's hands clenched the rim of the suitcase, the anger he'd succeeded in suppressing up to that moment just barely within his control. "My God, Ava," he bit out. "I know I've been a fool where you're concerned, but just how big a fool do you take me for? I saw the rushes of your love scene with Derek. It's pretty damn obvious you're still in love with him."

"That was acting, Kirk," she insisted, leaning toward him. "Believe me, that's all it was."

"I think I'm qualified to know something about acting, so I also know the real thing when I see it." The image of Ava's face after Derek had kissed her flashed in his mind, sending raw pain slicing through him. "If you could have seen your face when you looked at him. It was... radiant with love."

"It was *acting*," she insisted again. "I was merely recreating the way I felt about him once. And as I was reliving those feelings I suddenly realized that I'd been more in love with love than I was with Derek." Reaching out impulsively, she put her hand on his.

Kirk stiffened at her touch. He meant to pull away from her, but he couldn't. He was caught by the emotion suffusing her wide green eyes, making her parted lips tremble, soft and unbearably sensuous.

"Kirk, what you saw up there on the screen was just a young girl's fantasy of love. A love that was romantic, perfect, painless... and unreal." A rueful smile flickered across her exquisite face. "Real love isn't that easy. I know that now. It shakes you to the core and changes you in ways you've never dreamed."

"Tell me about it," he blurted out.

Ava's breath caught as she realized that that was the closest Kirk had come to admitting he loved her. Her hand tightened around his. "If you know what I mean then you *must* feel the same way I—" The shrill sound of the telephone cut her off, making her jump.

It freed Kirk of the spell she'd woven so expertly around him. Pulling away from her, he stepped over to the night table and lifted the receiver in the middle of another demanding ring.

"*Pronto?* Yes, Marco." He shook his head impatiently. "No, I didn't realize it was that late. It's a good thing you called." He checked his wristwatch. "Twenty minutes? Okay, I'm going to have to push it, but I'll be ready."

"Kirk, please, you can't leave," Ava pleaded before he'd even hung up. "There's no reason for you to leave." She jumped to her feet. "Derek and I aren't lovers. The rumors you've heard about us aren't true. You've got to believe me!"

The very real anguish in her voice held him back for a moment. He had to remind himself what an exceptional actress she was. "Even if that's true," he told her evenly, "it doesn't change a thing." Brushing past her, he started toward the dresser to get the last of his clothes. "You may not have gone to bed with Derek, but you're still in love with him."

"No, I'm not," she protested, following him over to the dresser. "That's what I've been trying to tell you."

His only response was a raw curse when the drawer jammed as he was pulling it open roughly. He wouldn't even look at her.

"Kirk, please try to understand," she implored. "I was so devastated when Derek left me, I shut love out of my life completely and buried myself in my work. But part of me,

I realize now, still wanted love desperately. So I clung to the only thing I had left, the memory of my first love affair, and I turned it into this fantasy of perfect love.''

"I know all about it," Kirk reminded her grimly. He'd given up on the impossibility of trying to compete with her fantasy lover. Scooping up the entire drawerful of undershirts and briefs in his arms, he began carrying them over to the bed.

"Then I met you, and you turned my whole life upside down," Ava went on, keeping step with him in spite of his long impatient strides. "For five years I believed I was in love with Derek and in one night you shook my fantasy world to pieces. I felt so confused, and you were right, I *was* afraid of you...of the feelings you'd aroused in me."

Ava halted by the foot of the bed and waited for Kirk to say something, but having just dumped all his underwear into the suitcase he was busy straightening it out.

"If you'd once told me you loved me," she added accusingly, "I might have felt differently. But you didn't."

He finally turned to face her. "Ava, I tried everything with you. Nothing worked." His tone was just as accusing as hers. "You wouldn't give me a chance. I tried to give you the most beautiful wedding a bride could have, so you'd always cherish the memory of our first day together as husband and wife, and it meant nothing to you."

"But why didn't you tell me that? I thought it was just a publicity stunt."

"And this villa, and the honeymoon plans I made, were they just publicity stunts? They meant as little to you."

"You're talking about *things*, Kirk," Ava cried. "You showered me with beautiful expensive things, but you never told me how you felt about me."

"I thought I showed you how I felt about you when I made love to you," he tossed back bitterly. "But you threw that back in my face, too, the next morning."

"That's not true." Unzipping the side pocket on her jumpsuit, Ava removed the jewelry box she suddenly remembered having placed there that morning. "*This* is what I threw back at you. Another one of your extravagant gifts." She thrust the velvet box in his hand. "And you can't imagine how cheap it made me feel!"

"Cheap?" Kirk snapped the box open, revealing the exquisite emerald pendant. "How could this possibly make you feel cheap?"

"All right," she amended, "not cheap, expensive. Like a high-priced call girl."

Kirk stared at the emerald pendant for a long moment, trying to see it through Ava's eyes. For the first time, he tried to imagine what her feelings must have been when she woke up the morning after he'd made love to her to find him gone, a gift in his place. *Payment for services rendered.*

"You're right," he murmured almost to himself. "Only it wasn't sex I was trying to buy, but your love." With a wave of his hand, he indicated their opulent surroundings. "All of this, everything I did, was an attempt to get you to love me."

"You wanted *my* love, Kirk," Ava said ruefully, "but you weren't willing to give me *your* love in return."

A tiny vein twitched violently in his jaw. "Because I knew you didn't want my love."

"How could you know that when you never offered it?"

"I did...with this!" He thrust the emerald pendant practically in her face. "And when you rejected it, you rejected me!" Snapping the box shut, he slammed it down on the night table, unable to tell her that the gift was his attempt to show her how much he loved her. "I know I may not have said what I felt in so many words but..." His attempt at an explanation trailed off, ending on a sigh of frustration.

"It only takes three," Ava reminded him softly. She counted them out on her fingertips. "I ... love ... you."

His face hardened and he turned away from her again. Slowly, calmly—almost too calmly—he finished packing.

"You can't say them to me even now," she persisted. "Can you?"

"Jesus Christ, Ava, leave me something!" Kirk exploded. "You've taken everything else! My pride, my self-respect, the joy in my work, which was the only thing I cared about until I met you!" No longer able to contain the pain and anger he'd been suppressing for so long, he turned on her. "You actually expect me to stand here and tell you I love you when I know you're in love with Derek?"

With one furious swing of his arm he sent the suitcase sailing off the bed, halfway across the room, scattering clothes in all directions. Ava gasped, and her mouth went dry with fear. She wanted to get out of range of the anger that was coiling every muscle of his powerful body and the potential for violence she sensed he was barely able to control, but she couldn't move.

"Do you also want me to tell you what it's been like for me this past month?" He moved in on her, driven by the intensity of emotions he was past controlling, his voice raw. "Night after night I waited for you to knock on that door, but you never did. Every single day I had to watch you with Derek and pretend it wasn't eating me up alive knowing that you wanted to be with him instead of me. Why the hell do you think I went to Rome the day you did the love scene with him?"

"Your business meeting," she stammered.

"There was no business meeting." Suddenly the anger drained right out of him. Pain flashed in the depths of his eyes. "Just the thought of Derek touching you, kissing you as he used to was enough to tear me up. I was afraid of what I might do when I saw you and him—" His words broke off.

As Ava watched in stunned silence, Kirk drew in a long breath and let it out slowly. "For three days and nights I walked the streets or drank myself blind in my hotel room, trying to put off coming back here to see the rushes." He shook his head as though his behavior were so foreign to him he still couldn't accept it. "But since I'd caused enough talk by not being there when the most important scene in the film was being shot, I knew there was no way I could get out of seeing them."

He paused, the memory clouding his eyes, darkening them further. "Well, I saw the rushes all right." He made an attempt at a laugh. It came out in jagged pieces that cut right through her. "I saw the love in your eyes when you looked at Derek. I heard it in your voice when you told him how you'd always loved him. I guess I went crazy with jealousy, I don't know. I lost control in front of everyone." Shame and humiliation burned on his face, thinned his lips to a hard white line.

"Kirk, I . . . I'm sorry." Tears filled Ava's eyes and her voice was barely audible. She hurt so deeply for him she could hardly breathe. Longing to make it up to him for the pain she'd unwittingly caused him, she reached out to him with both hands.

"Don't!" Kirk warned, anger flaring dangerously in him again. "I don't want your pity. Just get out. You got what you came here for, didn't you?"

She swallowed convulsively and shook her head. Her lips parted as though she meant to tell him something but was unable to. A single tear slid down her face.

With a curse, he started to move past her, but she stepped directly in front of him. She was so close he almost bumped into her, so close he caught that elusive scent he'd always found arousing because it mingled so perfectly with her skin. He wanted to grab her arm and pull her to one side so he could get by her, but he couldn't trust himself to so much as touch her.

Sarcasm was the only defense left him. "Isn't your ego satisfied yet? What more do you want? I told you how much I love you, isn't that what you wanted?"

"Yes!" Another tear slipped past her lashes as she threw herself into his arms. "That's all I've ever wanted!"

Kirk staggered back, caught off-balance as much by Ava's words as the impact of her body crashing into his. Before he could recover, she'd wrapped her arms around his neck, drawing his face down to hers. Her mouth stifled the protest he'd started to utter. He meant to push her away but his anger unraveled at the feel of her and he grabbed on to her, instead, pulling her even closer. When he felt her lips open invitingly under his, he thrust his tongue deep inside her.

An uncontrollable shudder went through Ava. Unlike the cool seductiveness of Derek's kiss, Kirk's kiss was all heat and hunger, almost bruising in its intensity. And when he put his arms around her, it wasn't to hold her in a perfect embrace but to crush her to him as if he meant to make her part of him. He was as helpless to resist the desire raging through him as she was.

The phone rang several times before either of them was aware of it. It rang a few more times before they dragged their mouths away from each other's, sharing the same reluctant sigh. Then Kirk released Ava and, stepping over to the night table, yanked the receiver off the hook.

"Yes?" He had to make an effort to get his breath back—as well as his reason. He'd never felt more confused in his life. "Yes, Marco, I know how late it is," he managed, "but I'm not ready yet." He'd completely forgotten about his flight. Judging from her sharp intake of breath, so had Ava.

While he listened to Marco going on about traffic snarls and airport security, Kirk watched Ava intently. She held his gaze with wide, imploring eyes. Eyes that gleamed unnaturally bright, as if she were on the verge of tears again. Her face was flushed, her lips wet from his kiss and softly swollen.

He wondered how he'd ever believed he could leave her.

"I can't possibly make that flight then, Marco," Kirk informed him. "I still have some important matters to take care of first. Please call and cancel for me, will you? Thanks."

The audible sigh of relief that escaped Ava left Kirk feeling more confused than ever. He replaced the receiver slowly. "I don't understand any of this."

"It's very simple," Ava told him with a tremulous smile, able to breathe again now that she knew he wasn't leaving. "I love you."

"What about Derek?"

"Didn't you hear anything I said to you before?" she cried. "I don't love Derek anymore. I'm not sure I ever did."

"But the rushes," he insisted, unable to let go the images that burned indelibly in his mind. "I saw your response to him when he kissed you. I don't think I could ever forget it."

"Kirk, Derek asked me to marry him a little over an hour ago," she admitted, going over to him. "If I still loved him, would I have refused? Would I be here with you, instead?"

He didn't bother to conceal his amazement; he couldn't have if he wanted to. "You refused to marry Derek?"

"Yes. And as for my response to his kiss, was it more or even as much as my response to your kiss just now?" She smiled softly, lovingly. "I didn't see the rushes, but I know it couldn't have been, because I never felt this way with him." She moved closer. "I didn't really know Derek any more than he knew me. We never touched except on the most superficial level." She moved closer still, the tips of her breasts grazing his chest. "But I didn't know that until *you* made love to me. I didn't know what love was until *you* showed me." Her arms went up to circle his neck and she looked deep into his eyes. "Show me, Kirk. Show me what real love is."

With a strangled cry, he brought his mouth down on hers and wrapped his arms around her tightly, striving to gather her all up, to surround her with himself. He kissed her over and over, deep devouring kisses that left them both shaking, clinging breathlessly to each other.

"God, I love you, Ava," he muttered fiercely when he'd lifted his mouth from hers. "Don't ever doubt that again. I've never... hell, look what I'm doing to your chin," he added regretfully. "I have to shave."

She laughed raggedly. "No, I don't mind." Her hand moved to rub the scratchy stubble on his chin, then smoothed the lines of exhaustion etching his rough face. Tired and unshaven, his hair a mess, he looked more beautiful to her than Derek ever had—or ever could.

"And I have to take a shower," he added with a reluctant sigh.

"No, you don't," she assured him. Lowering her head to the opening in his shirt, she buried her face in the rough silk of his hair and breathed him in deeply. The natural male scent of his skin was far more arousing than any men's cologne. Her tongue flicked out to taste him.

He groaned and every powerful muscle in his body stiffened. "I'd better make that a cold shower."

Her head snapped up in surprise. "A cold shower? Why?"

"Because I want you too much." He reached down to pull her hips tightly against his. She gasped when she felt his male heat burning through the layers of their clothing.

"I'm so hungry for you," he grated in between tiny stinging kisses on her mouth, "I could throw you down on that bed and take you right here and now. But I don't want to do that—not yet." With long strokes of his tongue he soothed away the tiny stings, sending shivers through her. "I'd like to slow things down a bit."

Laughing breathlessly, Ava threw her head back. "This is not the way to do it."

"You're absolutely right," he agreed, but he took her mouth again in a long ravenous kiss, dissolving her. He was shaking as much as she was when he finally released her. "Come and take a shower with me."

Ava hesitated. "Not a cold shower?"

"No, a hot shower." He laughed, a deep sexy laugh that was also a promise. "A very hot shower."

Twelve

Dropping their clothes carelessly onto the mosaic floor, they undressed slowly, searchingly, as if discovering each other for the first time. With only the lightest of caresses they touched each other's naked body, seeking to prolong the sense of wonder each found in the other.

Using long delicate strokes, Kirk's hands glided over Ava's luxuriant hair, from the top of her head down to her waist, skimming the soft curves lying just beneath. "You'd better do something with your hair," he suggested, "or it'll get soaking wet."

"I can wrap it up in a towel," she said, but her fingers continued tracing the vibrant, shifting muscles in his back.

"Do that." His hands closed over her breasts and he felt their budding tips straining through the silky blue-black locks covering them. "I don't want anything getting in my way when I touch you."

"No," she agreed, her nails raking over him, "nor do I."

A sudden impatience seized them both. Pulling away from her abruptly, Kirk hurried over to the circular glass stall to ready the water for their shower. Tugging a bath towel out of one of the antique brass rings embedded in the white marble wall, Ava quickly wrapped the towel into a turban around her head.

He was waiting for her, soap in hand, water streaming down his powerful torso and muscular legs, when she stepped into the shower stall. With one motion, he slid the frosted glass door closed and pulled her into the water with him. She gasped when she felt his heated flesh on hers.

"Isn't that the right temperature?" he asked.

"Perfect," she breathed, but she wasn't referring to the water.

Holding her securely against him with one arm, he turned her around so that the warm spray of water cascaded down her back. Releasing her, he began working up a rich lather between his palms.

With long, caressing motions his hands slid the thick foam over her delicate throat and shoulders, then up and down the length of one arm, raising goose bumps. One by one, he soaped each finger. Just as slowly, as thoroughly, and with the same result, he lathered her other arm and fingers.

He took his time working up fresh soapsuds, his eyes moving over her breasts as though he were trying to determine his plan of attack. A smile flickered across his face, and he handed her the soap.

Ava's fingers tightened around the bar of soap when Kirk filled his hands with one breast. Using circular movements, he smoothed the lather over every curve, leaving only her nipple free of the creamy foam. With long wet strokes of his tongue he washed the rosy peak until tiny cries shivered out of her. His hands were shaking when he soaped her other breast and his mouth closed over the swollen peak that time, drawing it into the heat of his mouth.

With barely controlled hunger he tugged on her, letting her feel the softness of his lips as well as the sharp sting of his teeth. She had to grab on to the towel rack on the shower door to keep from slipping. The sound of the water cascading behind her, misting their bodies, was like a roar in her head as wave after wave of the most intense pleasure broke over her.

"This is how I'd like to start every day with you," Kirk said when he finally lifted his mouth from her. His tone had been teasing, but the look in his eyes couldn't have been more serious. Taking the soap, he quickly worked up more lather before returning it to her trembling hand.

With slow strokes his fingers traced the delicate line of her ribs and glided down her narrow waist, over the soft curve of her stomach. She could feel the heat of his skin through the thick foam, the hungry pull of his hands as they moved over her. The low sounds he made at the back of his throat told her of the pleasure he found in touching her, intensifying hers.

Kneeling before her, he lifted her leg and placed her foot firmly on top of his knee. With both hands he swirled the creamy lather around her thigh, his nails raking the sensitive inner part, leaving a trail through the suds, before he slid more foam down the length of her calf and foot. When he'd finished doing the same to her other leg and foot, he released her and straightened. She didn't know how she was able to stand, in spite of the brass rack she was still clinging to.

Taking a step back, Kirk admired his handiwork. His gaze moved down her body as thoroughly, as heatedly, as his hands had, lingering on the gleaming black mound between her thighs. He smiled crookedly. "I seemed to have missed a spot." Swiftly his fingers moved to tangle in the short, damp curls, making her gasp. "Can't let that happen. I want to feel every part of you." His gaze darkened, became deeply possessive. "Every inch of you...inside and out."

Ava's breath caught at his words, then tore out of her with a moan when she felt his fingers sliding on her with long rhythmic movements, opening her up searchingly, slipping deep inside. Her hand tightened convulsively around the towel rack, making the glass door shudder in its frame.

"You're so incredibly soft and warm," Kirk groaned. "Like hot silk." He shut his eyes tight to block out every sensation beyond the burning, melting feel of her. For Ava, all reality had narrowed down to his touch. For endless moments he caressed her, his breath shortening with every stroke. Her own breath had become part of the roar in her ears, indistinguishable from the sound of water cascading down her back, the blood pounding at every pulse point in her body.

He had to pry her fingers loose to get the bar of soap out of her hand. "Turn around," he ordered thickly.

"Kirk, I...I don't know how much more of this I can take."

"Turn around."

Shakily she obeyed him, shifting her hold on the towel rack to her other hand.

His strong, warm hands soaped her nape, then massaged her shoulders, dissolving the last remnants of tension that remained from her sleepless night. But she could feel a different kind of tension coiling ever tighter inside her. When he'd finished soaping her back, after lingering erotically over the soft curves of her bottom, there wasn't an inch of her body that wasn't covered with thick, creamy foam.

"Talk about icing on the cake," he said with a low sexy laugh when he turned her around to him again. "You look like you're covered in whipped cream." He lowered his mouth to within a breath of hers. "You look good enough to eat."

"That's not fair," Ava protested raggedly, twisting her head away before he could kiss her. "Haven't you ever heard of equal time? When is it my turn to soap you?"

"Right now." His arms went around her, pulling her up against him. Skin sliding wetly on skin, he rubbed her all over him, transferring the soapsuds from the front of her body to his. She gasped when she felt the wiry curls on his chest scraping against her tender nipples, felt him pressing, rigid with desire, against her own aroused flesh.

"No," she moaned. "Don't. It's not fair. I want to touch you, too."

He went very still and his eyes narrowed as he searched hers deeply. "Do you?" he asked, with a strange catch in his voice.

"Yes," she breathed, longing to give him as much pleasure as he'd given her. "Oh, yes."

Anticipation made her palms tingle when she rubbed the soap between them before handing it to him. With the seriousness of a person performing a task for the first time, she carefully spread the lather along the strong column of his throat and down over his powerful shoulders and arms. She loved the feel of his water-slicked muscles tightening at her touch, the contrast between their hard strength and the smoothness of his skin.

With growing fascination she explored every line and curve of his broad chest, feeling the uneven rise and fall of his breathing under her palms, his heart beginning to beat stronger and faster. Eyes half-closed, she slowly traced the differences between his body and hers.

Burrowing her fingers into salt-and-pepper hair that felt like raw silk, she discovered the flat male nipples hidden within. She smiled, very pleased with herself, when she felt the tremor that rippled through him as she slowly circled them with the tips of her fingers until they were as taut with desire as hers.

"You like that, too," she murmured. His reply was a deep growl. Bending her head, she licked off the drop of water that hung, quivering, on one nipple before she drew it into her mouth. Her hands never stopped swirling the foamy lather over his torso while she tormented him with teeth and tongue.

A groan tore out of Kirk. He was amazed that she would want to do that for him, and deeply moved. A rush of love such as he'd never known for any woman went through him when she lifted her face and looked up at him. She had soapsuds on the tip of her nose and chin. Her face was flushed and her eyes were like fiery emeralds, aglow with the sensuality she was only beginning to discover in herself.

"I love to touch you," she admitted, her voice a husky murmur, her hands sliding down his body.

He swallowed past the tightness in his throat. "I love to have you touch me."

She laughed suddenly as her finger traced his navel. Impulsively she leaned down and dropped a kiss in his navel. He dropped the soap.

She laughed again and went down on one knee to retrieve the bar of soap, and quickly foamed up fresh lather.

The soap flew out of her hands when he bent down and grabbed her, hauling her back up to him. "That's enough of that," he grated, his mouth reaching hungrily for hers.

"But I'm not through yet," she protested, evading him.

His fingers dug into her shoulders. "Do you know what you're doing to me?"

"I hope it feels as wonderful as what you do to me." Softly, lovingly, she brushed his lips with hers. "I never knew anything could be so wonderful." With a hunger only he had ever evoked in her she kissed him deeply. One hand went up to tangle in his damp silvery hair, the other rushed eagerly down his body to make further discoveries.

When she found his aroused flesh her fingers trailed lightly, tentatively over him. Slowly she explored him, like a world that was all new to her, and full of wonder. She'd never known that the mere act of touching could be so erotic. Her hand closed over him, surrounding him. A violent shudder went through him and he threw his head back as his whole body went rigid with pleasure. She could feel his excitement grow as she continued to trace his male potency, his velvety softness heating the soapsuds under her hand.

Her name was a hoarse cry as he crushed her lips with his and his arms locked around her, pulling them both into the cascade of water. With deep hard thrusts of his tongue Kirk filled Ava's mouth, anticipating how he would soon fill her body. Water poured down over them, sliding between their bodies, stripping them of the lather, while steam swirled around them.

"God, I'm dying for you," he got out between clenched teeth when he tore his mouth away from hers.

"Yes," she breathed, meaning she felt the same way.

Barely taking time to turn off the water, Kirk lifted her out of the shower. Swiftly he unwound the turban from around her head, sending her hair flowing down her shoulders and back in shimmering black waves. She'd assumed he meant to use the towel to dry her, but he tossed it impatiently onto the mosaic floor, instead.

Drops of water gathered and slid down her body as he swept her up in his arms and carried her quickly into the bedroom. Without bothering to turn down the covers, he spilled her onto the quilted bedspread. She shivered as she felt cool satin against her heated flesh. His body came down on hers, all wet and slippery and smelling fresh as summer rain.

He took her mouth again in a quick, fierce kiss, sliding between her legs more roughly than he'd intended, then drank the moan that rippled out of her when she felt him burning against her, melting her. His arms tightened around her, crushing her to him as he searched her face intently. "Do you want me?"

She wanted him so much she could barely breathe let alone speak. All she could manage was a nod.

That wasn't enough for him. With deliberate, agonizingly slow strokes he moved against her, letting her feel his heat and hardness, how very much he wanted her. The effort it cost him to hold back shot tremors through him that ricocheted deep inside her. "Tell me how much you want me." His voice was raw.

Her hips arched wildly against his, answering his need and hunger with her own, and when she was finally able to put the words together they came out in pieces. "I never knew I could want anyone this much."

He entered her with one deep powerful thrust, making her cry out, then held her, unmoving, barely breathing, until the shock wave of their coming together had washed over them.

"Open your eyes, Ava," he urged. "Look at me."

Her eyes fluttered open, dazed and bewildered.

"I want you to see that it's *me* making love to you, not some fantasy lover." Holding her startled gaze as possessively as he held her body, he began moving inside her. "I want you to know it's me you're feeling!"

"Oh, Kirk," she gasped, "but I do—" The rest of her words shattered into incoherent sounds as he thrust deeper and deeper inside her, splintering her with an intense pleasure she'd never felt before.

She'd meant to tell him that not even in her wildest fantasies had she dreamed such passion existed, that nothing had ever felt more real to her than him. He was all that there was of reality, and all she would ever need. Nor had she ever felt more intensely alive, her senses filled to overflowing with him, and every atom of her being vibrating with the ecstasy only he had ever brought her to.

Unable to tell him with words, she sought to tell him with her body as she opened herself to him utterly, daring to give him everything, holding nothing back. The hard groan that ripped from him, the shudder that convulsed him told her of the pleasure she gave him, filling her with a joy she'd never known.

Wrapping her arms and legs around him, she urged him closer, deeper, until he filled all of her and she was surrounding all of him. As one they caught fire and burned in the same flame, consumed by an ecstasy that swept them beyond reality, beyond fantasy, beyond everything.

For several long minutes they clung together until their heartbeats and breathing returned to normal and the world took shape around them once more. Then Kirk shifted his body, lifting only his weight off Ava while remaining close to her, within her, and he looked deep into her dazzled eyes. "I always knew it would be this way with you."

"I never knew anything like this was possible."

He smiled crookedly. "Not even in your fantasies?"

"No," she breathed. "I never dreamed such love existed." Her face was radiant as she looked up at him, more radiant than he'd ever seen it, blinding him.

"I'll make all your dreams come true, Ava," he vowed.

"You already have, Kirk." She twined her arms around his neck and drew his head down to the soft, fragrant warmth of her breasts. "I could never want more than this."

Long after they drifted off she held him, reluctant to let go, even in sleep, the love that exceeded her wildest dreams.

Silhouette Desire

COMING NEXT MONTH

BRIGHT RIVER—Doreen Owens Malek
Jessica's father had thought that Jack Chabrol had been an unacceptable suitor for a daughter of Bright River's wealthiest family. Could love temper Jack's bitterness when fate brought Jessica back?

BETTING MAN—Robin Elliott
Kate Jennings could make book on the fact that Griff Hayden was perfect for her ad campaign. Griff was determined to convince her that all bets were off when it came to love.

COME FLY WITH ME—Sherryl Woods
Who was that man following Lindsay Tabor around Los Angeles Airport? However preoccupied Lindsay may have been, Mark Channing wasn't a man she could easily ignore.

CHOCOLATE DREAMS—Marie Nicole
Keith Calloway was a man with a mission, and satisfying the world's cocoa cravings was priority number one. But vivacious Terri McKay quickly had this serious-minded man dreaming of forbidden treats.

GREAT EXPECTATIONS—Amanda Lee
Megan couldn't share her secret with anyone, least of all Greg Alexander. Her project was too close to bearing fruit to blow her cover—yet she knew Greg could deliver the dream of a lifetime.

SPELLBOUND—Joyce Thies
According to Denise Palmer, Ph.D., Taggart Bradshaw was a stress-prone type A and therefore Mr. Wrong for her. So why was Taggart bent on showing Denise just how right he could be?

AVAILABLE NOW:

THERE ONCE WAS A LOVER
Dixie Browning

FORBIDDEN FANTASIES
Gina Caimi

THEN CAME LOVE
Nancy Gramm

JUST JOE
Marley Morgan

STOLEN DAY
Lass Small

THE CHALLONER BRIDE
Stephanie James

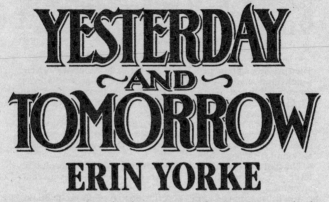